NEVER AFTER

DAMAGED HERO

KELLY MOORE

Edited by
KERRY GENOVA

Illustrated by
DARK WATER COVERS

NEVER EVER AFTER

NEVER EVER After

BESTSELLING AUTHOR
KELLY MOORE

Copyright © 2023 by Kelly Moore

All rights reserved.

No part of this book may be reproduced in any form or by any electronic or mechanical means, including information storage and retrieval systems, without written permission from the author, except for the use of brief quotations in a book review.

❀ Created with Vellum

1 NOA

"Are you working on your food blog?" Sofia tips her head over and brushes her long, wavy, mahogany hair.

"Could you maybe not do that near my coffee?" I pinch my fingers, picking up one shiny strand from the table. "And no. I'm working on something different."

Her hair flies as she swings her head up. "Whatever it is, it's good to see you focusing on work rather than…"

"The tragedy of my life," I cut her off.

"That's a bit dramatic," she mumbles, then continues. "You're concentrating on the past instead of your big, bright future. You do realize our restaurant opens in two days?" She lifts two digits.

"The Fork and Dough." I sigh.

"It's going to be the best pizza joint in all of Massachusetts." She removes the band from around her wrist and ties her hair in a knot on top of her head, then rummages through the fridge. "We really need to go buy groceries." She twists her neck to look at me. "Are you not eating again?"

"The thought of breakfast these days makes me nauseous. I'll stick to coffee."

She pops the lid off a yogurt container and snatches a spoon out of a drawer, and sits across from me with one knee drawn up. "What are you writing?"

"I thought I'd share some tidbits about my life struggles, and perhaps it would help others who might be floundering to find their footing."

"Alright, it might serve to get you out of your funk. Read me what you've got so far."

"Really?"

"Yes, really. We're sisters. If you can't share it with me, how are you going to put it out there in the world?"

I press my lips together to stifle the dryness. "I only have a few words written down." I read from my laptop screen.

"The last two years, my world has consisted of one pertinent word: *After*.

After my husband died.

After his funeral.

After I found out the man I loved had an affair.

After I found out he had a son.

After his restaurant closed.

After the apartment we shared sold.

After I met someone else…

Then the ultimate nail in my coffin…*After* Ever."

I PAUSE, studying my screen.

"Is that it?"

I nod.

"What comes after Ever is a partnership with your sister. We purchased this quaint cottage on the ocean with a magnificent view, and we're starting new chapters of our lives. Happy ones. I have every confidence that you'll meet someone new."

"I don't want just anyone. I want Ever, but I can't have him."

"Then you need to resolve to truly let him go. You know it's for both of your own good."

I snap my laptop closed. "You're right," I appease

her, knowing he's the man I'm always going to carry in my heart.

She digs her keys out of her purse. "I'll be at the restaurant taking care of last-minute business. Are you going to come by later?"

"Yes, after I finish my food blog." She knows damn good and well I'm going to go back to my life blog.

"Did you and Ever have unprotected sex at any time?"

I scowl. "What kind of question is that?"

"You said the thought of breakfast makes you nauseous." Her brows raise.

I stare at her, dumbfounded.

"When was your last period?"

"I…um…" I squint, thinking hard. *Did we have unprotected sex?* The night I found him in his office on the yacht. I start counting back in my mind. I can't be. My periods have always been irregular. "Ever wore protection," I lie, not wanting to think about the reality of the one time he didn't.

"Perhaps you should run by the drugstore and pick up a pregnancy test."

"You're making something out of nothing." I shoo her out the door. "Shit." I pop open my calendar, trying to recall my last period, gnawing on a poor innocent nail. "Three months." The same length of time it's been since I left him. My head falls to my keyboard. *After Ever*...a rush of tears burns my eyes.

My cell phone vibrates across the table, and I still can't answer it without holding my breath first, wanting it to be him. I whimper when my mother's face lights up my screen.

"Hi, Mom."

"How is my beautiful girl?" Her accent isn't as thick as it used to be, but it's still there.

"I'm good." The second lie today, and it's not even nine o'clock. I don't want her to worry about me anymore. She was the glue that held me together after Drake died. She doesn't need to be put through any more of my heartache. Not that losing my husband was easy by any means...it was awful, but he was dead and never coming back. Ever is out there somewhere living a dangerous life, and even though I told him I didn't want to see him ever again, I can't stop thinking about him...dreaming of him...longing for his touch...craving how he made my body feel beneath his.

"Are you still there?"

I close my eyes, shaking off my thoughts. "Yeah, I'm sorry. What were you asking me?" I haven't told her about Ever, but she suspects something more than losing the restaurant happened.

"I was just saying, I know you've been struggling since you lost The Italian Oven, but I'm so proud of you and your sister for opening a restaurant where you both grew up. It's going to be such a success. I've invited everyone I know to the opening."

"Thanks, Mom. I appreciate it." Ines Laurant is not the type of woman who sits by idly and doesn't lend a hand when needed. She's totally devoted to her family, and after all these years, she still thinks my father hung the moon, which he has for all of us.

"Perhaps you'll meet some handsome man."

I exhale. "I'm not really interested in meeting anyone."

"Oh, sweetie. At some point, you need to move on."

"I have, Mom."

"Did you do what the therapist suggested?"

"It's on my agenda today."

"Do you want me to go with you?"

"No. I need to go alone, but I appreciate your support."

"When you get there, if you change your mind, call me, and I'll be there."

"Thanks, Mom."

"Tell my baby girl I love her," I hear my father yelling in the background.

"Love you too, Dad," she tells him for me. "I really need to get going if I'm going to make it to help Sofia later."

"Just remember how much you're loved."

"Love you, Mom." I hang up and give up the idea of writing anymore this morning. Grabbing the keys to my convertible Mustang, I let the top down and back out of the driveway.

The day is as sunny as they come and warm. The road winds around the grassy coastline to the cemetery. After Drake was killed, I had him brought back here so I didn't have to go to New York to talk to him whenever I wanted. I haven't been here since I found out about his affair. My therapist suggested I deal with my last bit of anger. She thinks it's what's holding me back, but she doesn't know about Ever. The only person that knows about him is Sofia, and she pinky swore to me, like we used to do when we were kids, that she wouldn't mention him to anyone. He's my secret, and sometimes I think I imagined him. He crashed into my life so fast and hard that he took my breath away, but one thing is for sure...I'll never, *ever* be the same.

Shifting gears, I turn into the cemetery and drive

to the very back, where his headstone overlooks the ocean.

"Hi," I say softly, tracing his engraved name in the marble. "I'm sorry I haven't been here in a while, but a lot has changed. I've changed." I pause and remove my sunglasses and shield my eyes with my hand. "I've been so angry with you. How could you cheat on me and then hide the fact that you had a son?" I sit with my legs crossed in the grass. "I met both of them. Of course, I hated the sight of her and the excuses she made. What ticked me off was her telling me how much you really loved me," I scoff. "If you truly loved me, I wouldn't have been sitting face to face with the woman you had an affair with and giving her your life insurance policy money to raise your son." My eyes remain dry, but my voice carries in the wind.

"If you wanted another woman, you should have ended things with me first! You owed me that, if nothing else! I tried to justify it because I was gone so much, but I would've never cheated on you!" I aim a finger at his grave as if he can see me. "Looking back now, our relationship was never what I thought it was." My voice lowers to a hush. "I know this because I met someone who filled every part of me. I wasn't aware I was missing anything until him."

Tears blur my vision. "It doesn't really matter now because I've lost him, too, and the ironic thing is, it's because of you. Of all the people in the world for me to fall in love with, his family is responsible for your death. I want them to pay so badly, but in the end, it will only hurt the man I've given my heart to."

I get to my feet. "This isn't a tit-for-tat thing. You had an affair, and I tell you about him. This is me moving on from both of you. I'm done being angry. I miss the man that was my first love, not the man who cheated on me. Your son, who looks like you, by the way, will be taken care of. Bruno and Gia will make sure of it." Fitting my sunglasses snug to my face, I turn to walk away. "One more thing." I spin on my heels. "I lost the restaurant." It's an admission that's still hard for me to make. "I thought you should know."

A large boat off the shoreline catches my attention, and I walk over to the fence line, staring at the horizon. "Ever," I whisper his name like a prayer, longing like hell for it to be him, but it's not. I clutch my hand to my aching chest. "God, how I wish things could be different." Inhaling, I turn around, make my way to my Mustang, and cry what I can only hope is the last tear I will shed.

I speed through the curves of the road and don't

slow down until I come to the downtown area of Essex and park behind the small building we've rented to house The Fork and Dough. We had a tough time finding a place, and neither one of us wanted to buy property in case it didn't work out. Besides, I still have a bad taste in my mouth from the ordeal with Drake's restaurant.

Sofia is squatting close to the floorboards, painting them a bright white color. "Hey," she says, blowing a tendril of hair that escaped her bun out of her eyes.

"What do you need me to do?" I ask, tucking my purse behind the cherry wood counter.

"The wine should be arriving at any moment. We need it inventoried and some of the bottles displayed on those shelves." She points with the paintbrush.

"Did you hire an assistant manager?"

"I did, and he's meeting me here at two."

"He?"

"Yes, and he's easy on the eyes." She waggles her brows.

"I thought you didn't mix business with pleasure?" I laugh.

"I don't, but you, on the other hand, could use someone to help you forget Ever."

That's not going to happen. "I'll pass."

"You haven't even met him yet. He's totally your type."

I launch my hand on my hips. "What pray tell is my type? I mean, Drake and Ever couldn't have been more different."

"How about someone in between their personalities? Drake was sweet and driven and Ever reeked of danger from the beginning."

He was a danger to my heart. "I think I just need to focus on myself and not bring anyone else into my life."

"Speaking of bringing someone into your life, did you go by the drugstore?"

"I'm not pregnant," I huff. "I've been extremely stressed, and I've never been regular. I'm sure any day now, I'll get a visit from my friend."

"I'll pick up a pregnancy test on my way home," she mutters.

"You aren't going to let this go, are you?" I squint one eye at her.

The door opens with a man pushing a dolly loaded with a stack of boxes. "Where would you like these?" he asks and then smiles at Sofia.

"I'll show you," I say, and he follows me into the storage room behind the kitchen. "You can just set them here."

He unloads them and pushes the dolly out, and stops to grin at Sofia again before he marches out.

"You're always on me about finding a man. What's your excuse?" I prop my hands on my hips.

"I'm too busy to be in a relationship."

"Come to think of it, have you had a serious relationship? I remember in high school you had the hots for the quarterback. Whatever happened to him?"

"He joined the military, and when he came back, he was never the same. He ended up marrying the girl that sat behind me in math class. Last I heard, they moved out West and have a couple of kids."

"No one since then?"

"It will take an amazing man that will let me be me for me to fall in love."

I was more myself with Ever than anyone else. "Same here." As I say the words, I ponder. Who am I really? The only answer I have is that I belong to Ever. Everything else seems meaningless to me, other than my family.

2 EVER

My father is pacing the floor of the boardroom, rambling on about future acquisitions and how to go about obtaining them under legal pretense. Nick is glued to his every word, and Victor sits across from me with a permanent scowl lodged on his forehead every time he looks at me. He's still pissed off that I beat the crap out of him when I saw him leaving Noa's apartment. That was three months ago.

Three months of agony.

Three months of pure torture trying to convince my father that this sick family comes first.

Ninety days of paying my dues for crossing Carmine Leone.

He tested me by ordering the execution of a man

who double-crossed him in a deal. I met him at the docks with no real intention of killing him but to encourage him to leave New York permanently. He had other plans and wanted to take out one of Carmine Leone's sons, preferring it to be Nick, but I was the one that showed up. The memory of taking his life gnaws at my gut, even though it was in self-defense. It sickened me to take advantage of the situation and boast to my father that the job was done with photographic evidence.

In doing so, I gained his trust, and somehow Nick felt it bonded us. He's backed off his hatred for me, but it's fueled mine for him. The deeper embedded I get in this organization, the better chance it gives me to take them down.

"We do have a potential problem brewing," my father states and leans his palms on the oval table. "Carmichael has been forced to step down due to some…let's say…indiscretion with a minor. Which means there'll be a new chief of police in the interim until our mayor appoints a new one."

"That shouldn't be an issue with the mayor in your pocket," Nick chimes in.

"The problem is, no one within the department is qualified, so he's filling the temporary seat with a man from an outside metropolitan area, and we know nothing about him." He walks behind me, digging his fingers into my shoulder. "Your task is to ensure he supports our organization."

This could be the break I've been waiting for. He's not been bought and sold to the Leones, at least not yet.

"His name is Trace Bentley. He's been working for eight years in the Buffalo area under the direct arm of their chief of police, who has a good relationship with Carmichael, so I can only assume he'll fall in line."

Not if I can convince him otherwise. "I'm sure with a little guidance and bribery, he will. I'll set up a time to meet with him."

"I trust you to handle it." He slaps my shoulders and then moves on to what he needs from Victor, who continues to glare at me.

"Why don't you let me handle the chief of police?" he snarls. "I know you trust your son, but I don't."

"You're just pissed that he beat the shit out of you." Nick chuckles.

"This is my organization, and I'll choose who does what. He's more than proven himself. He sacrificed the girl for us, and we made a mint off of her building."

Victor launches to his feet. "I think he's playing you!"

"Sit the fuck down and shut up or you're going to find yourself buried in a shallow grave gasping for air," my father admonishes him.

Victor jerks his jacket together and runs his hand through his slick-backed black hair. His narrow, close-set eyes are icy cold, and his large nostrils flair. "Don't say I didn't try to warn you."

"You focus on the jobs Nick assigns you, nothing else," my father snaps.

Victor growls before he settles down.

The face of my phone, that's sitting on the table next to my glass of water, lights up. I take a quick look and see a call coming in from Luca. "If we're done here, I need to take this." I point to my phone.

"I've wrapped up what you need to know." He waves me off, and I pick up my things and push through the glass doors to my office, calling Luca back.

"Have you laid eyes on her?" I ask, closing the blinds.

"No, sir, not yet. We've just docked offshore from the Essex Marina."

"Whatever you do, don't let her see you. Keep your distance, but make sure she's safe. Victor is suspicious, and if he thinks for one minute that I have anything to do with Noa, he'll go after her."

"Hence the reason you bought another boat. Noa would've recognized it if she saw it."

"I'll fly there this weekend under the pretense of a business meeting. But I might have just found a way out of all this mess. I can't give you any details, but I'll fill you in when I see you."

"Do Noa and Sofia have any idea that you're the owner of the building they rented for their restaurant?"

"No. I made sure my attorney only listed my company name. And if she was ever to search, she'd find a fictitious name. This goes for my father too. He'd know right away I've been lying to him all this time."

"Are you going to show your face at their grand opening, sir?"

"I'll be there in disguise."

"Do you think that's a good idea?"

I don't give a rat's ass…I need to see her. "She'll never know it's me." Every part of my being wants to say fuck it and run away with her, never be found. It wouldn't be fair to her to ask her to leave her family behind and not risk seeing them again. I want a life with her so badly I can taste it, and I'm willing to walk through hell to make it happen. She's the life preserver that gets me through the mucky waters of my life whether she knows it or not. The things I've done the past three months have all been for her…to keep her safe.

I've kept my fake apartment, spending my nights on the yacht. My sheets still smell of her, and every time I open my drawer and see the handcuffs, it makes my dick hard. It doesn't take much. The difficult part has been pretending that I'm interested in other women. I smile on the outside when photographers at events snap pictures of me with a woman on my arm, only to cringe on the inside because the skin I'm touching on the small of their backs isn't Noa's skin. As soon as the events are over, I send them on their way. No more midnight walks of shame for them. I want nothing to do with any of the phony pleasantries or women wanting what's underneath my belt for the money they think it can bring them. Noa ruined me for all other women. None of them come close to being who I need and desire in my bed.

"I'll purchase a car like you instructed as soon as the boat is anchored to the shore."

"Make sure the window tint is extremely dark. I don't want her seeing you watching her."

"I'm well aware of how much you want her in your life, sir, yet I'm worried it will cost you yours."

"If I can't have her, I have no life anyway."

I hear his deep exhale. "Alright. I'll keep an eye on things here and report back to you."

"Thank you, Luca. You're a good friend."

I stuff my phone in my pocket and run around to my desk, picking up the receiver of my office phone when there's a knock on my door. "Come in," I say, and cover the phone with my hand.

"I need to discuss a project with you." Nick saunters in, holding a file.

"Sorry for the interruption. Please schedule me in his calendar as soon as he's settled." I hang up.

"You're a man of your word. Our father would be glad to know you're on top of things when it comes to the new chief of police." His entire demeanor has changed toward me, believing I'm a murderer like him.

"The sooner we know we can control his actions, the better off our family will be." My gut is tangled in knots.

"I'm glad we are on the same page." He sits, tossing the file on my desk. "We have, let's say, an associate who is trying to back out of a deal he made with us. Victor is tied up on another project, and I'd like your help."

Opening the file, I scan it. "Where did our father get his hands on these types of explosives?"

"He's got deeper pockets than either one of us knows. He's worked for this type of deal his entire career. Everything else is pocket change in comparison. If this deal falls through, there will be hell to pay."

"Did you know he expanded into explosives? Why aren't we keeping our priorities on land acquisitions and laundering money?"

"Are you that naive or blind?"

I crane my head to the side and stare at him.

"The cargo you sell and ship in containers are weapons for the cartel and rogue agents."

"I always assumed it was drugs."

"They're smuggled into the weapons."

Shit. I could go to prison for life. "What is it you need from me?"

"This guy, Stanley Turro, and I butt heads. He doesn't care for me, and the feeling is more than mutual. I need you to be levelheaded and win him over."

"That explains why you don't want Victor involved."

"I have a meeting set up with him for you next week when he's in town. Schmooze him, whatever it takes, but this deal has to go through. If not, his family will find his body parts all over Manhattan, according to our father."

"Tell me the time and place."

"I'll text you the information." He stands. "You can always resort to torture if blackmail doesn't work. I have every detail of his life mapped out for you in those papers, with his weaknesses highlighted."

This family will stop at nothing to get what they want. "I'll handle it."

He struts to the doorway of my office. "I'm glad we're on the same team. It beats the shit out of hating your guts."

I plaster on one of my forged grins. "Ditto."

As soon as he clears my office, I pull out a flask of bourbon from my desk and twist off the cap, taking a long swig. The burn down my throat eases the throbbing of my temples. All I can think about is Noa, and how to get out of the mess I'm in.

"Perhaps, I can introduce Stanley Turro to Trace Bentley." I peruse the file Nick left for me, and I find he's done a thorough job. I could use his weaknesses to get what I want…my family behind bars. If this is the only way my father will ever pay for my mother's death and Nick for killing Drake, among others, then so be it.

Picking up the phone, I call the police department, arranging an appointment with the interim chief of police. It's set for Tuesday, and my meeting with Turro is Wednesday. I put my plan in motion. The one thing I haven't been able to get my hands on again is my father's log. I broke into his safe late one night only to find it empty. I need it to prove the acts of crimes he's committed.

"It has to be in his house." I rest back in my chair, twirling a pen between my fingers. "Nick has to know where it is. He's second in charge and would have to know where the evidence is to burn it if something were to happen to our father," I mumble to myself.

Getting up, I make my way to my father's office and tap my knuckles on the wooden door. "I scheduled a meeting next Tuesday with Bentley."

He peers over his reading glasses. "Nick filled you in on my other priority?"

"Yes."

He points to the chair for me to sit.

"Three months ago, I was ready to write you off. You've come a long way since then. You would've shit yourself knowing that I'm moving explosives."

"It's a good financial move." What I really want to say is that I can't wait to see him behind bars. I lean forward, placing my elbows on my knees, and my chin rests on my folded hands. "How did you go from asset management to laundering money, to drugs, to explosives?"

"It's all about the connections you make, Son."

I loathe it when he calls me son.

"I've amassed a lot of power over the years, and I'm a very persuasive man."

Meaning he'd kill you if you didn't do what he wanted.

"But I'll let you in on a secret." He gets up, closing his office door. "I've…let's say, twisted the arm of a higher-up in the military, and he was happy to provide me with whatever I needed."

The interpretation of that is he threatened someone the higher-up loves. It's the only reason I'm sitting in his office. People will do anything to protect their loved ones. Thankfully, he thinks I'm not truly capable of loving anyone so much that I'd sacrifice myself for them. "Never let it be said that Carmine Leone doesn't get what he wants." I stand, glancing at my watch. "I wanted to let you know I'll be out of town this weekend. I'm headed to LA. There's a piece of property I think I can get my hands on for a steal and turn a good profit."

"You can handle that over the phone."

"It's going to take a bit more negotiating than a phone call, if you get my drift."

"Ah, you truly are coming into your family name. When are you going to officially change your last name to Leone?"

Fucking never. "I'll speak with my attorney on getting the paperwork drawn up."

"You could have saved yourself a few scars had you been obedient when you were younger."

I want to rip his throat out with my bare hands. "Yeah, I was a stupid kid."

"Try to have a little fun while you're in LA. I hear the women are gorgeous but expensive."

"I plan on it." How many lies can a man tell in one day?

3 NOA

"Hey, Sis, can you take a break from inventorying and meet our new assistant manager?" Sofia pops her head into the storage room.

"Sure." I lie my tablet on a shelf and follow her to her office.

"I'd like you to meet Ricco Bonetti."

I swallow hard. She wasn't kidding; he's easy on the eyes. He has wavy jet-black hair with a tint of red at his temples and a freshly shaven jawline with a prominent dimple in his chin. He sports a smooth forehead other than a thick vein over his right eye. It makes him sexy as hell, not to mention his pearly whites. He has a slight hitch to his left eyebrow that turns upward. His body is brawny, and sculpted biceps bulge from under his short-sleeved shirt.

"It's a pleasure to meet you." He smiles and shakes my hand.

"Where are you from, Mr. Bonetti?"

"Ricco, please. If we're going to be working together, we should be on a first-name basis."

"Okay, Ricco, where are you from?"

"Originally from Italy, but I've lived in Boston since I was six years old with my mother."

"What type of experience do you have?"

"This isn't an interview. I've already hired him," Sofia snorts.

"It's alright. I don't mind. I managed a modest-sized Italian joint in Cambridge. Prior to that, I worked my way up learning every aspect of the restaurant business."

"Why would you want to go from being a manager to an assistant position?"

Sofia's pencil-shaped eyebrows pinch together, glaring at me.

"What? It's a reasonable question." My shoulders gather toward my ears.

"And one that I've already asked him. Do you not trust me to hire an assistant?"

"It's really okay. I simply wanted a change of pace

from the city. I'd been to Essex several times while vacationing and fell in love with the town. I was very upfront with Sofia that one day I'll want to open my own place, but for now, I'm happy with a few less responsibilities."

"Sounds like my sister has found the perfect person for the job. I'm sorry about the inquisition."

"No worries. I understand you're a food critic."

"Was, past tense. Now I write food blogs."

"Among other things," Sofia murmurs.

"I'm more of a silent partner. Sofia is the restaurant expert."

"Oh, so you won't be around much." His brows sink.

"Only when necessary to help out, like opening day."

"We are expecting half the town to show up in support," Sofia adds.

"If it would be alright, I'd like to treat you ladies to dinner in celebration of The Fork and Dough's success."

"I'd like that. It will give the three of us a chance to bond." Sofia wraps her arm around my shoulder.

"Would tonight work for you ladies?"

"Sounds good to me. How about you, Noa?"

"Why not?" I relent, knowing I'll get an earful from her if I say no.

"I'll make reservations for three at the marina restaurant. I hear it's the best place in town for seafood."

"I love that place." Sofia claps.

"It's a date then." He takes out his phone and calls the restaurant.

"Isn't he gorgeous?" Sofia says, dragging me into the kitchen.

"Admittedly yes, but I'm not interested. He'd be perfect for you, though. You have the love of a good restaurant in common."

"As temptingly scrumptious as he is, we'll be working together, nothing more."

"Suit yourself." I shrug and go back to the storage room to finish the inventory. An hour later, I find myself in Sofia's office, and she's slamming her laptop shut. "What are you hiding?" I ask, walking around to her side of the desk.

"Nothing." Her voice gets a high pitch when she's lying.

"Show me." I cross my arms over my chest.

"Seriously, it's nothing for you to worry about."

"The last secret that was kept from me cost me the restaurant."

"Oh, sweetie, it has nothing to do with The Fork and Dough. You know everything there is to know. No secrets."

I lean down, flip up her screen and tap a button for it to light up. I gasp when there is an article on Ever. The picture attached has a redhead hanging on his arms and looking into his eyes like she wants to devour every inch of him.

"Are you keeping tabs on him?" My mouth gapes.

"Only so that I know his whereabouts. You're safe if he stays in New York."

I stare at the photo, and my heart literally hurts. "How could he move on so quickly? I've been moping around for three months, and he has a gorgeous redhead drooling all over him."

"Seems to me he's forgotten all about you and returned to his old ways." She runs her hand down my arm, trying to comfort me. "It's a sign that you should do the same thing."

"Just because he's moved on doesn't mean I'm over him." I take a closer look at the photo. "His facial expression is fake, and he's not even looking at her the same way she is him."

"Stop making excuses to be alone."

"I don't need a man to make me happy."

"Then be happy! I dare you!"

"Ugh," I rasp and stomp out of her office like a petulant child. "I'll see you at the cottage later." I bolt out the door and head back to the house, changing into my running clothes and shoes.

With earbuds in place and my playlist blaring, which is the one that Luca told me is Ever's favorite, I hit the sandy beach. As my feet slap the dry sand, the sound I can't drown out is Sofia's words. "Be happy. I dare you." I can plaster on a smile like Ever did in that picture, but will I be happy again? The only answer I can come up with is...no, not without him.

I stop breathlessly and yank my phone out of the side pocket of my running shorts and scroll, finding his name. I type a text,

I MISS YOU SO BADLY. *You've wrecked me for anyone else.*

MY FINGER LINGERS over the Send button a few seconds before I hit it. Standing in place, I wait to see the three little dots, and my heart sinks when they don't appear. I'm so lost and confused without him. I face the water and scream. "I can't take any more pain!"

I succeed in startling a flock of birds that fly off. I grip my phone and look one more time before cramming it back in my pocket and taking off in a full run, finding myself at the marina. For some reason, it brings me a measure of comfort.

Eyeing an empty bench, I sit and watch a large boat maneuver into a spot at the end of the dock. It's the one I saw earlier and wished was Ever's. Briefly closing my eyes, I see myself back on his yacht, bound by him in handcuffs, touching every part of me, inside and out. He claimed me that night and I him. What I'd give to go back to that day and disappear with him in the sunset.

My phone vibrates. My heart lurches as I tug it free from my pocket, holding my breath, willing it to be Ever. I release a deep sigh seeing a text from my father.

DAD: *I'm taking the boat out tomorrow. Do you want to go fishing?*

I respond, *I'd love to.*

Dad: I'll pick you up at eight.

. . .

THE LAST TIME I fished was with Ever. Maybe going with my father will help me erase the memory. Checking the time, I get up and jog back to the cottage. Hitting the shower, I wash quickly and wrap a towel around my chest and search for something to wear. I look up on the shelf above my clothes and see the bag I stuffed the letter in that Luca gave me before I got on the plane back to Essex. I've not been able to open it.

"Today is the day," I say, stretching on my tiptoes to pull out the letter. I sit cross-legged in the middle of my closet. My name is written in Ever's handwriting on the outside of the envelope. Sliding my finger under the tab, I slowly peel it back, opening it. Inhaling courage, I unfold the letter.

NOA,

YOU'RE MY HEART...THE *only woman that I've ever loved. It wasn't something I planned, nor wanted, but I couldn't stop myself. I wish I would've had more self-control when it came to you.*

. . .

I SHOULD'VE SENT *you away the first night.*

I should've never pursued you when you left my bed.
I should've stuck to our deal of no attachments.
I should've walked away from you.

I KNOW *that's a lot of should haves. I got so lost in you that I forgot who I was, what family I belong to. If I could change it, god knows I would. My family is as dirty as they come. I've fought like hell to run from them, but there's no escaping my blood unless I can find a way to tear them down one by one. The sound of that makes me a monster like them.*

I desperately want something I can never have...and that's you. I can't ask you to enter my world, and I don't want you part of it. Loving me puts you in danger and I will die before I let them hurt you.

Know this, somehow, some way, I'll find my way back to you. My life is meaningless without you. But, your life has to have meaning. You're a beautiful, strong woman who has survived a nightmarish trauma. Not knowing who killed your husband haunts you, and if I ever find out who it is, I'll make sure they pay.

. . .

"HE HAD no idea at the time it was his own family," I whisper and continue reading.

YOU'VE GOT *no idea what it's been like growing up in a world of lies, violence, and so much corruption. I'd choose any life but mine. I'd say I'm sorry that I fell in love with you, but I'm not. You've given me something to hold on to and to see a different future for myself, one that I desperately want, yet unable to have. Thank you for loving me with all my flaws. I know that we can't be together, but I'll always carry you in my heart. I feel better knowing you're safe away from me...for now.*

I WONDER if he still feels this way. He wrote this before the truth came to light.

"Noa! Are you in here?" Sofia's voice rings out.

Folding the letter, I stuff it back in the bag and walk out of my closet. "Yeah, I went for a run, and I'm trying to find something to wear."

"How about that pale blue sundress you bought when we went shopping last week. And maybe do something pretty with your hair." She flings a tendril of wet hair off my shoulder.

"This isn't a date," I say smugly.

"That doesn't mean you can't look extra nice."

"Meaning I don't usually look nice?" I huff and return to my closet.

"That's not what I'm saying at all. I just think it would be fun for us to dress up a little and have a good time."

"That's all well and good, but let me make myself clear. I'm not interested in Ricco." The hangers scrape across the wooden bar, and I find the blue dress.

"I understand." She waves in surrender. "I'm going to go get changed."

I stare at the letter from Ever, wishing like hell it was him I was having dinner with tonight.

4 NOA

The seafood restaurant is a local dive that fills up on the weekends and frequently sells out of lobster before the dinner hour is over. This place has been here for as long as I can remember. I brought Drake here a few times, and it made him have second thoughts about serving seafood rather than Italian food. In the end, he wanted to stick to his roots, but he loved coming here.

Ricco is waiting outside with his phone pressed to his ear. He hangs up when he sees the two of us strolling hand in hand. "You ladies look gorgeous." He smiles, showing his perfect teeth.

"We're a bit too dressed up for this dive," I snort.

He's wearing a pair of casual khakis and a deep green pullover that works well with his olive-colored skin. "Our seats are waiting on us," he says, holding open the door. "I hope you don't mind, but I requested a table on the outside patio. It's a beautiful view and a nice evening."

"It's perfect." Sofia smiles, and we stroll through the packed restaurant.

"I'm surprised you were able to get us a table," I remark.

"They had a last-minute cancellation, and I booked it." He pulls out my chair and then Sofia's.

Ever would have written a big check to have the place emptied for the two of us, is where my mind goes. Ricco takes a seat between us and tucks his phone into his pants pocket. "You ladies have eaten here before. What do you recommend?"

"Lobster," we say in unison.

"The oysters are good too." Sofia smacks her lips as if she can already taste them going down.

Does everything have to remind me of Ever. Sitting on the balcony of his boat, eating oysters. "I like the fried calamari with the pepperoni in them.

"How about we order all three." He grins.

The waitress comes over to take our drink order. "Two mango margaritas with sugar on the rim and extra tequila," Sofia tells her.

"I'll have an ice-cold lager, whatever you have on

draft."

A beer guy, not bourbon with a round ball of ice. As if Sofia read my thoughts, she jabs my shin with the toe of her sandal. "They have a great selection of IPA beers behind the bar."

"We'll order our appetizers while you're here," he tells the waitress. "Two dozen oysters and a basket of calamari."

"You should really go ahead and order the lobster, too, before they are sold out," Sofia says sweetly.

"Alright, three lobsters and…" He scans the menu. "A large basket of crab legs to go with it."

"That's enough food for an army," I murmur.

"You'd be surprised at how much food I can consume." He rubs his tight abs.

"You must work out all the time." Sofia flips her hair over her shoulder and beams.

She's flirting with him. I mean, who wouldn't under normal circumstances. All the women in the restaurant are gawking at his good looks.

"I take it you're not married. There's no sign of a ring on your finger." I point to his left hand.

"Nope. I've never found the right woman, and in my…our line of work, you know how hard it can be when you're married to your business."

"That's for sure," Sofia snorts. "There are days I can barely find time to shower, much less find time for a man."

I'd say Drake and I made it work, but we didn't. We led separate lives, and look where that got us. Would we still be married if he was still alive? This question has plagued me for the past couple of months. Would I have even given Ever a second look? His affair would have eventually come out, and that would have ended us for sure. So, was I destined to meet Ever?

"How about you?" He aims his question at me. "I assume you're married or have been by the faint discoloring of your ring finger."

"I'm a widow."

"I'm so sorry," he says.

Our drinks arrive just in time. "Let's make a toast to a successful venture." Sofia raises her margarita, and we all clang our glasses.

Out of the blue, I feel like someone is watching me. My brows crease as I scan the area.

"Are you alright?" Sofia asks from the corner of her mouth.

"Yeah, I'm sure it's nothing." I wave her off but continue to glance around.

Sofia and Ricco make small talk until our food

arrives on a platter. "These look delicious," Ricco states, placing his napkin in his lap.

I try to enjoy the evening even though I can't shake the feeling that I'm being watched. Is it Ever? Is he out there somewhere in the distance, keeping an eye on me? Snagging my phone from my purse, I send him another text that will probably go unanswered.

ARE YOU WATCHING ME? *If so, I want to see you.*

"EVERYTHING OKAY?" Sofia scowls.

"Yes, I just forgot to answer Dad about fishing tomorrow." There I go lying again.

"Just goes to show that you're his favorite." She sips from the rim of her glass. "He never invites me to go fishing with him."

"That's because you hate fishing, and you never shut up, scaring the fish away."

"True." She laughs. "How about you, Ricco? Do you like to fish?"

"Being the son of a single parent, it's not something my mom took me to do, so I can't say one way or the other if I enjoy it or not."

"What happened to your father?" Sofia asks, and I nudge her under the table.

She jumps, and he chuckles. "It's alright, but I don't have a good answer for you. He was never in the picture."

Sounds like Ever's father.

"Do you have any idea who he is?" Sofia can't help herself.

"No. My mother has never spoken of him, and the one time she did, she simply said we were better off without him.

He could literally be kin to Ever. "Probably some mafia type," I mutter, and he stares at me for a long moment.

"Possibly," he finally states.

"Enough of this seriousness." Sofia slurps an oyster. "We should make this a monthly routine. The three of us meeting here and celebrating our wins."

"I can handle that." Sofia cheers again.

The band starts playing, and Ricco wipes the corner of his mouth. "Would you like to dance?"

It takes me a second to realize his question is directed at me. "No, I'm um…good, thank you."

"Oh, come on," Sofia whines. "Loosen up a bit and have some fun." She literally shoves me out of my seat.

Ricco places his hand on the small of my back as we walk around the tables, and it takes everything in me not to push him away. The only hands I want on me are Ever's.

He extends his arm, so I tuck my hand into his and brace my other hand on his shoulder, and we sway to the music. "This is nice," he mewls.

"Yes." I rub my lips together, peering over his shoulder so I don't have to look him in the eye.

"I know we've just met, Noa, but I really like you and your sister. I think this is all going to work out perfectly."

"Business wise, you mean?"

"Of course, but if something were to develop between the two of us, I wouldn't be opposed."

I drop my hands and take a step back. "Let me make myself very clear. I have no interest in anything other than a working relationship with you."

"Ouch," he says, laying his hand over his chest. "That's a blow to my ego."

"I'm sorry. It's not meant to be. My heart belongs to someone else."

Sofia jumps between us. "My turn," she says, and I return to the table, still aware that someone is watching me.

Sofia and Ricco return to the table, all smiles, as the lobster and crab legs arrive. We all delve into cracking open the shells and bantering back and forth. I'd swear Sofia has a thing for him. Perhaps I should warn her he hit on me, but why burst her bubble.

Sofia orders another round of drinks, but I barely sip on mine. Ricco downs four more beers with his meal. My sister excuses herself to the ladies' room, and I'm left at the table with Ricco.

"I want to apologize for what I said earlier. It was very presumptuous of me, and I'd never interfere with another man's woman."

I feel bad. "It's alright. You had no idea."

"So, we're good?" He toggles a finger between the two of us.

"Yes. All is forgiven."

"Good," he says, polishing off his last beer.

He pays the tab, and we all walk down the long dock. My sight shifts to the boat from earlier. "I wonder who owns that." I point.

"Somebody very wealthy," Sofia scoffs and locks her arm with mine. "I think I might have had one too many margaritas." She holds up four fingers.

"Thank you for dinner," I turn, saying to Ricco. "I'm going to get her home."

"It was my pleasure. I'll see you ladies tomorrow at the restaurant." He opens the passenger side door, and Sofia slithers inside. He moves to open my door.

"I can get it. Thanks again for dinner." I get behind the wheel, and as I'm buckling up, I watch him take out his phone and make a call before he disappears into his dark Yukon. Why would a single man drive an SUV and not some sports car?

Sofia, in her inebriation, turns up the volume on the radio, sings at the top of her lungs, and puts down the convertible top. She bellows until we're parked in the gravel driveway of our cottage.

"Alright, Adele, it's time to go to bed," I snicker and help her out of the car.

"Ricco is so handsome." She bats her eyes.

"I don't think you're going to be able to have a hands-off policy with him," I say, dragging her into the house.

"Oh, I almost forgot," she slurs and slings her purse on the table. "I stopped at the drugstore and bought you a pregnancy test." She whips it out of her bag.

"I'm not pregnant," I protest.

"Prove it," she says with one eye shut.

"Let's get you in bed." I drag her to her room and take off her sandals when she flops on the bed.

"I didn't think I had that much to drink." She's already curling into a ball with her pillow tucked under her head.

"You've always had a low tolerance for anything other than wine." I kiss the side of her head and pull the comforter over her. "Good night, Sofia."

"Good night." She hiccups and closes her eyes.

I walk back into the living area and stare at the pregnancy test on the table. "Even if I am, I'm not ready to deal with it," I say, leaving it on the table and stomping into my bedroom.

"HI, DAD," I greet him at the door, and he kisses both of my cheeks. My father, Franco Laurant, values his traditional Italian heritage. He was born in Italy, but his family immigrated to America when he was only a small boy. His mother and father insisted on speaking Italian only at home when he was a child, so he still carries a thick accent. He comes from a rather large family of four boys and two sisters that are scattered up and down the East Coast of the United States. Even though there is distance between them, they've all remained very close. I grew up with lots of aunts, uncles, and a multitude of cousins. My father was very hopeful when I married Drake that I'd fill our house with children and disappointed that we didn't. He didn't hold back his feelings about the two of us living in different places most of the time. He said it wasn't good for a marriage, and he was right. But not once as he ever said, I told you so. He's shown me nothing but love and respect.

Sofia complains I'm his favorite. In a way, I think I am. I'm more like our mother, and he adores her. Sofia was a bit bratty as a teenager and gave him a hard time. He loves her, but she's been his challenge. I know his only regret is not having more children. My mother miscarried several times after me and said she couldn't go through the heartache anymore and was blessed with two beautiful daughters. I'm sure my father would have loved to have a son, but it wasn't in the cards for them. He gathered me on his hip and did all the things with me you'd do with a boy, and I ate it up. He's taught me things I will always be grateful for.

"Are you ready, *neonate*?

His baby girl. I still love it when he calls me that. "Let me snag a light jacket so I don't get sunburnt."

"Your *madre* packed us a picnic," he says, holding up the basket.

"Please tell me it's pasta and freshly grated parmesan cheese."

"And her *cannoli fatti in casa*."

I laugh. "You really need to decide if you're going to speak Italian or English."

He shrugs. "Why not *entrambi*?"

"Okay, Dad, both," I snort, and we head out of the house.

"I was *pensado* we could take your auto."

"We can take my Mustang. I know how much you love to feel the wind in your thick hair." I pop the trunk, and he puts the picnic basket in it and then grabs our fishing gear.

"Is the johnboat already at the marina?"

"*Si*, I dropped it off *Ieri*."

"Yesterday." I giggle. I think he knows the right words but insists on keeping me on my toes. He knows I can speak fluent Italian and French. Both of my parents made sure of it.

"Okay, Papa, let's get you buckled." He smiles, loving when I call him Papa rather than Dad. I climb behind the wheel and let the top down, and he instantly starts playing with the buttons on the radio.

"What's this?"

"It's a playlist," I tell him backing out of our

driveway.

"What's a *elenco di riproduzione*?"

"It's a compilation of favorite songs."

"Ah," he says and pushes the button, and we listen to Ever's playlist on the way to the marina.

"Why such heavy songs, neonate?" He frowns.

"They belonged to someone else."

"A *uomo*?"

"Yes, a man," I answer softly.

"No Drake?" Sadness fills the crevices of his eyes.

"No, Papa, but there's nothing for you to worry about. It's someone I met in New York when I visited Sofia."

"You love him?"

I shift the car into park. "It doesn't matter because it was never meant to be. Some stories aren't meant to happen."

"*Amore* is always meant to be." He squeezes my hand.

"Not this one, Papa." He's always been a big believer in romance. He's constantly doing some romantic gesture for my mother even after being married for thirty-six years. He'd never understand my relationship with Ever. To him, Drake hung the moon, and I'd by no means want him to think otherwise.

5 EVER

I shuffle out of my suit jacket and hand it to one of my staff members. "I need an update," I tell Luca.

"Why don't you wind down with a drink first?" he says, pouring me a glass of bourbon.

I throw it back and slam the glass on the bar. "Consider me wound down."

"I'm not sure you're going to like it, sir." He shoves his hands in his pockets. "And I don't like spying on Noa."

"This is the sole reason I had you dock this boat in the marina. I know it's not as big and comfortable as the yacht, but I couldn't bring it here."

"It has nothing to do with the size of the boat, sir."

"I can't keep her safe if I don't know what she's up to." I run my hand through my overly long hair.

"She's safe as long as you stay away from her. You being here risks her life."

"I've taken every measure to ensure my family doesn't have any inkling that I'm in Essex."

"I know you love her, but I still think you should let her go."

I pick up the glass and throw it at the wall. It crashes into several pieces on the wood floor. "I can't! She's the one thing in my life that's good!"

He lets out a heavy sigh. "Unfortunately, I agree with you. I just hate to see you risking both of your lives."

"Tell me what you've seen." I sit on the couch in front of the computer screen, knowing he's been instructed to record whatever he's found.

He sits beside me and opens a file on the screen, and pushes Play. "This one captured her running, nothing else."

How can he say it didn't capture anything but her running? The way she moves and the rise and fall of her chest has me aching immediately. "What else?"

"This is from last night. Noa, Sofia, and a work associate had dinner on the pier."

"Who the fuck is he?" I growl, pointing at the screen.

"He's the man that Sofia hired as the assistant manager of their new restaurant."

"What's his name, and have you done a thorough background check on him?"

"Ricco Bonetti. He's from Boston, and I'm still working on his credentials. Nothing suspicious has come back yet."

I keep watching the video, staring at Noa's beautiful face. She rarely smiles, and if she does, it's at her sister. I ball my hands when she steps on the dance floor with Ricco.

"This is the part you're not going to like," Luca stammers.

"He means nothing to her. Look at her body language. She's appeasing him, or perhaps her sister." I turn it off when Sofia trades places with Noa in Ricco's arms. "Where is she today?"

"She's fishing with her father not far from here."

"At least she's enjoying her day."

"Do you want me to drive you to where they are, sir?"

"We need to go over some business first. Let me get out of these clothes, and we'll talk on the upper deck." The boat is half the size of my yacht and doesn't have as many conveniences, but it will do the job. Two of my staff members, along with the captain and Luca, reside on the boat. Luca has set up my cabin and purchased the things I will need while I'm here. I went to the extra cost of purchasing tickets to LA in case my father had any suspicion at all because of Victor's mouth. I boarded the plane and then exited when no one was paying attention.

Changing into a pair of jeans and a T-shirt, I grab the sunglasses lying on my dresser and find Luca on the deck already waiting on me with a sub sandwich and a bowl of pineapple, along with a glass of sparkling water with lime.

"No bourbon." I chuckle.

"You need to keep a level head."

We sit at the small two-person table near the railing. "I've got a plan. Carmichael is out, and there's an interim chief of police. His name is Trace Bentley. He's not been bought and sold by my father yet. I have a meeting with him on Tuesday."

"What's your plan?"

"I'm going to offer him information that will take down my family."

"Where will that leave you?"

"If I play my cards right, a free man. I need to get my hands on my father's notebook, but I haven't located it yet. I need to come up with an excuse for Nick to tell me."

"Offer him women and an expensive bottle of whiskey, and he'll tell you anything."

"I'll make note of that. My father is dealing…" I stop mid-sentence. "Actually, you don't need to know what he's up to. It's a dangerous game he's playing. The man he made a deal with, Stanley Turro, is trying to back out of the deal. My father wants me to convince him otherwise at all costs. After I meet with Bentley on Tuesday, I have set up a meet and greet with Turro the following day."

"You're going to set them up," he says.

"If Bentley will play along, then yes."

"And if he doesn't?" He knits his brows together.

"I haven't gotten that far yet. It has to work. I have no other choice. The opportunity is now, or I'll not get my life back, or Noa."

"Bentley could throw you in prison with your family."

"That's a risk I'm willing to take. At least I'd be comforted knowing my family wouldn't be able to get their hands on Noa."

"As much as I hate to admit it, you're right. It sounds like your only way out."

"If something happens to me, I want you to steer

clear of New York. I've set up a bank account with your name on it. You'll never need or want for anything. You can go wherever you want in the world, just don't go back to the city. The same goes for Noa. I've set up a trust fund with her as the beneficiary. She'll probably be pissed, but I don't give a shit. I don't ever want her in a bad financial situation again."

"I don't think you have to worry about that, sir. She's levelheaded, and after what she experienced, I don't think she'd borrow money again. She and her sister have come up with all the capital they need to open their restaurant. And, thanks to you, they didn't need to purchase a building."

"That will also be deeded to her if I die or if I'm incarcerated."

"You truly love her, don't you?" He cups my shoulder in his hand.

"To the point where it hurts. I didn't think it was possible, but I can't deny it."

"I'll do anything I can to help you."

"You're already doing it. Take me to her." I stand.

"Before we go, there is one other thing." He gets to his feet and walks into the kitchen area, pulling open a drawer, and lays my old cell phone that I gave him on the counter. "I know you told me to get rid of this, sir, but I thought if Noa ever needed to contact you, this is how she would do it." I rise, and he pushes it in my direction.

"She called me?"

"Texted."

I open her message and draw air into my lungs with a deep inhale.

I MISS YOU SO BADLY. *You've wrecked me for anyone else.*

"I MISS YOU, TOO, BABY," I rasp, then read her next text.

ARE YOU WATCHING ME? *If so, I want to see you.*

"SHE KNEW you'd be watching her," Luca says solemnly.

"You will see me. You just won't know it." I turn the phone off and toss it back at him. "I need to see her now."

We walk down the steps of the boat to the vehicle

he purchased, and I climb in the front seat. "Good job on the window tint," I say. "Dark as shit."

The short drive around the curves of the ocean leads us to where there is a long dock filled with fishermen.

"There's a hat in the back seat." He hikes his thumb over his shoulder. "I'll grab the binoculars."

"Is she on the dock?" I question him before I get out of the car.

"No. She's on a johnboat near an island. You can see it from the end of the dock."

I get out and follow him, and several fishermen on the pier stare at us like we are out of place among them. Putting the hat on, I stand at the end of the dock, and Luca hands me the small binoculars and points. "Over there," he says.

I search for a moment before I find her and then sharply gasp. She's laughing as if she doesn't have a care in the world, and she's damn beautiful. "Lord, I've missed her," I whimper.

She stills and twists her head toward the dock like she's sensed me. I drop the binoculars to my side and level my stare into the water beneath me. "She can feel me," I voice to Luca.

"She can't see you this far out."

I lift my gaze behind my sunglasses to look at

her. She's shielding her eyes with her hand, peering toward us. I resist the urge to glance into the binoculars. They itch in my hand, and I want to raise them to my eyes. She finally turns back around in her seat, facing her father, and I take another look. "I'm going to make things right," I rasp. "Hold on, baby."

"She's safe for now. That's all that matters."

"Tomorrow is a big day for the Laurant sisters. I plan on being there."

"I have your disguise all set up. She'll never recognize you."

"Good. I feel like a stalker watching her, but I can't help myself."

"You are stalking her." Luca laughs. "Not in a bad way."

"Is Sofia at home?"

"No. She left for the restaurant early this morning."

"Take me to their place."

He twists his lips. "Are you sure that's a good idea?"

"No, but I'm going anyways."

"Alright," he huffs, and I take one last glance at her. "I love you, Noa, and I'm going to make this work if it kills me."

I follow Luca back to the car, and he drives the

short distance to their cottage. "I see why she loves this place so much. Why would anyone give it up for the likes of the city? It's so beautiful and peaceful. Her husband was a fool for dragging her away from Essex."

"Well, if he hadn't, you'd never have met her," Luca adds, shoving the car into park.

"There is that," I mumble. "Drive down the road out of sight. I'll call you when I'm done," I tell him, and then jimmy their front door open. I walk through the small living area seeing hints of Noa on display, then I find the room I know is hers and grab her pillow, inhaling her scent. Her closet door is ajar, and I can't stop myself from entering. Her clothes hang freely, and the dress she wore that night on the boat is on the end all by itself. "You looked so gorgeous I could barely keep my hands off of you. And, as I recall, I didn't."

Looking up, I see my handwriting on the envelope of the letter I wrote her. "Did you read it?" I breathe and take it down to see the flap has been opened. "Good."

Putting it back in place, I walk out onto their back deck overlooking the blue waters of the Atlantic. I can envision myself living here with her. I'd wake her up early, dance with her in the sunrise of the day, and then carry her back to her room and make love to her for hours.

My phone pings with a message from Luca.

SOFIA IS HEADED YOUR WAY.

I DUCK BACK INSIDE and into Noa's bedroom as the front door opens.

Sofia is talking to someone on the phone. "Yes, I had one too many drinks last night. That's not my usual MO," she tells whoever's on the receiving end. "I need you at the restaurant in an hour. We've got a lot of last-minute details to go over." She pauses and listens. "Yeah, Noa is not on the market to fall in love. She's had her heart broken one too many times." She listens again. "Alright, I'll see you in an hour."

I peek through the crack in the door, and she's rummaging in a cabinet, looking for something. "There you are," she finally says, pulling down a bottle of wine. "For the life of me, I couldn't recall your name." She tucks it under her arm and skates out of the house.

Peering through the window, I watch her back

out of the gravel drive and text Luca when the coast is clear. Scanning their living area one more time, I see a box on the table and move to check it out. "A pregnancy test," I rasp. "Is it hers or Sofia's?" I shove it into my pocket as Luca pulls up, and I skip out of the house, locking the door behind me. "That was close."

"Yeah, way too close for comfort."

"We should get back to the boat. I have some phone calls to make."

"You need to stay out of sight until you're in disguise tomorrow," he states as we pull up at the marina.

I get out and bound up the steps to my cabin, and open my laptop. I sent pictures of the property in LA to my father to cover my tracks, asking his opinion on my fake deal, knowing he won't want me purchasing land in California. He likes to keep his business within the northeast corner of the United States.

Once he's responded, I shut the laptop and take the test kit from my pocket. "Are you pregnant with my baby? If so, this changes everything." A tinge of blood spills in my mouth as I bite the inside of my cheek.

6 NOA

"What is it, neonate?"

"I don't know." It's the same feeling I had last night of someone watching me, but this feels more intimate. I shield my eyes from the sun and twist my body, scanning the shoreline. All I can make out is fishermen casting their lines into the water off the dock. I can't see faces, but I'd bet money that Ever is there somewhere.

"*Ho fame*," my father announces.

"I'm hungry too. Let's eat," I turn back around in the boat and dig through the picnic basket. "This has been just what I needed. Thank you for bringing me out here today." He's made me laugh, recalling one of our fishing trips out here when I was just a small girl. These are the times I treasure with my father, and I shake off the feeling of being watched, not wanting to share them with anyone. "I love Mama's pasta." I pour on an excessive amount of parmesan cheese and slurp up a noodle.

"*Fantastico*," he fills his bowl full of pasta. "Are you and your *sorella* ready for the opening?"

"Sofia is a perfectionist. I'm sure she'll have every detail in place. It's going to be a great success."

"What are you going to do?"

"Sit back and watch. I'm working on my food blog, and something personal I want to write. I'll work the opening, but beyond helping out every now and then, the place is hers to run."

"What's this *cosa personale* you are working on? I see a deep sadness in your eyes, neonate. Does it have to do with this uomo that listens to the sad songs?"

"Oh, Papa. I haven't been able to talk about him. Only Sofia knows the truth."

"You can tell me." He touches my hand with such tenderness I melt.

"His name is Ever Christianson, and I'm head over heels in love with him."

"Like Drake." He lifts a single brow.

"So much more," I admit with a sigh.

"I adored Drake, but I never saw that look in your eye like I have for your madre."

"Really? Why didn't you say anything; even remotely in passing?"

"If I would have, would it have stopped you?"

"No, I guess not. I thought I was happy. How could I have been so wrong?"

"Sometimes in life, we settle for things we think are good for us. This uomo, why aren't you with him?"

"It's a long story."

"I have time." He puts his paper plate down and stares at me.

"Ever is a good man in a bad situation. He doesn't have a loving, supportive family like I do." I pause.

"Go on," he encourages me.

"He grew up with his mother until she died when he was ten years old. He knew nothing about his father until then. Turns out he's a bad man, and his mother was trying to protect him."

"Mafia," he says without blinking.

"Yes, and Ever has been drawn into his family's world without his consent."

"But there is more you're not telling me."

"His brother is responsible for Drake's death."

He clutches his chest. "No."

"I left him because his family threatened to pin his murder on Ever and send him to prison for the rest of his life, if not worse."

"You left him to protect him."

"Yes."

"That, neonate, is true amore."

"Oh, Papa. I'll never find anyone that made me come to life like he did," I sniff.

"*l'amore trovera una via.*"

"Love will find a way. Do you really believe that?"

"With all my heart."

"I pray you are right, but I don't know how it's possible."

"You have to have faith. Your mother and I were not supposed to be together. My family believed in arranged marriages. All my siblings fell in place and married who was chosen for them. I fell in love with your madre the moment I laid eyes on her. My father forbid me from seeing her."

"Seriously, you've never told me this story. How did you end up together?"

"After only knowing her for two weeks, I asked her to marry me, and we ran away together to the courthouse behind my *padre's* back. He was furious."

"Nonno?" I widen my eyes. "What happened?"

"He gave up his wrath when he met her. He said

he couldn't have picked someone as wonderful as her. He didn't like that she was French, but she won him over."

"Wow!"

"When I thought all was lost with her, love found a way."

"I'm going to use that story in my blog."

"Be patient, neonate. You'll find your happiness."

"I love you, Papa."

He traps my face between his hands and kisses my nose. "*Anch'io ti amo.*"

He loves me too.

"What do you say we get back to catching some fish?"

I take one last bite of my pasta and tuck the bowl inside the picnic basket. "I'd like that." I smile an honest-to-goodness, genuine smile.

We end up catching three sea bass and four codfish before the end of the day. He drives the johnboat to the marina, and I get out and stand on the dock. My feet have a mind of their own when I wander over to the large boat moored on the end. I find it odd that it has no name on the stern. It looks new, so whoever owns it may not have had time to have the name painted on it. I can picture the name Ella written on Ever's boat and wish it was on this one. The captain of the boat steps out onto the bow and smiles at me.

I wave and want to ask him who the boat belongs to, but my father yells, getting my attention. "Noa!"

Glancing at my watch, I really need to get to The Fork and Dough, or Sofia is going to be in a tizzy. Turning around, I meet my father at my car. "Do you know who owns that boat?" My father tends to know all things concerning Essex.

"Only that it arrived a few days ago. The owner has asked the marina to keep the name private."

"Hmmm..." I mutter.

After dropping my father off, I run home for a quick shower. When I walk into my room, his scent slaps me in the face. "Ever," I speak his name. "I'm imagining things now." I shake it off and shower. As the water hits me, I peer down at my belly and run my hand over it. "I can't be pregnant, but if I am, I promise to always love and protect you, even from your father's family. If I have to live without him for the rest of my life, I'll do so to make sure you're safe." This must be how Ella Christianson felt when she ran away with her unborn son.

"It's time I find out." I turn off the shower and drape a towel around me and march into the kitchen. "Where is it?" I open a few drawers thinking

Sofia put it away. "It can wait until she comes home," I grumble and get dressed.

As soon as I walk through the back entrance of the restaurant, Sofia goes into a rant. "Nice of you to show up. I hope you and Papa had a great time." She plants her hands on her hips.

"Don't be mad. It was exactly what I needed."

It takes the wind from her sail. "Fine. Ricco and I have everything under control anyway. He's going to be fantastic at this job."

"I'm glad you're happy with him."

She drags me into a corner. "I really like him, more than I want to."

Do I dare tell her he was hitting on me while we danced? I decide against it. "You should tell him then."

She chomps on her fingernail. "I don't know. It's too soon, right?"

"You're asking the woman that fell in love with a man after one night in his bed," I snort.

"I just need to play it cool." She smooths out her silky top. "Let him come to me."

"I've not in any degree seen you so giddy before over a man."

"Me either." She splays her hand on her forehead.

"I'm being ridiculous. He's our assistant manager. I can't have feelings for him."

"Why not? You're a woman, aren't you? And he's a sexy man. I think you should go for it."

"I don't know. I should give it some more time."

"Suit yourself. What do you need me to do?"

"The chef arrived a couple of hours ago, and the place smells like pure Italian. Could you go over the menu and samplings with him. I want to make sure everything is perfect. He had some ideas for daily pizza specials. Just make sure they are in line with our goals as to what we want to serve our customers."

"Easy enough. By the way, when I went home to change, I was going to take the test."

She glares at my stomach. "The test?"

"Yes. I left it on the kitchen table last night. Did you put it away?"

"No, but perhaps when I went home to find a bottle of wine that I couldn't recall the name of, I knocked it on the floor."

"Alright. I didn't think to look on the floor. Did you find the wine?"

"Yes, and I've already ordered it, and they promised me it would be here first thing in the morning before we open." She grabs my hand before I walk away. "Do you really think you're pregnant?"

"I hope not. It would only complicate matters." *I hope so.* It would connect me forever with Ever, and I'd always have a part of him.

I walk by Sofia's office on the way to the kitchen, and I hear Ricco talking quietly to someone. "He's not here. There's been no sign of him."

Who is he talking to? I peek around the corner, thankful his back is to me.

"There is nothing else to report," he says on the phone, and I duck when he turns around. "I've gotta go," he blurts, and I tiptoe quickly into the kitchen to find the chef.

Who was he speaking to, and who hasn't he seen? Does he have anything to do with the Leones? Surely not. Sofia said she did a thorough background check on him. I'm sure it's nothing. I'm just being paranoid.

"Chef Andre. I'm Noa, Sofia's sister. It's so nice to meet you."

He kisses the back of my hand. "The pleasure is all mine."

"She wanted me to go over the menu with you and the daily specials you had suggested."

"Most certainly," he says and delves into his ideas as I sample the pizzas he's pulled out of the oven.

"These are the best pizzas I've ever put in my mouth," I say, catching a piece of stringy mozzarella dangling from my chin.

"From what I understand about your husband's reputation, that's saying a lot."

"His specialty was lasagna and other like dishes. He didn't serve pizza because there was a pizza joint around the corner from his place, and he didn't want to steal their business."

"Sounds like a good man."

"He was." Sometimes I forget the small things that he did that were nice for other people. That's the man I choose to remember.

By the time I get home, between the hot sun and working, I'm exhausted. I drop my purse on the floor, collapsing on the couch, and doze off, waking up when Sofia unlocks the door.

"Hey, I'm surprised you're not in bed." She hangs her keys on the hook next to the door.

"I thought you were leaving right behind me." I sit, rubbing my eyes.

"I was, but Ricco and I went out for a drink." She's all smiles.

"Did you tell him how you feel?"

"No, but I enjoyed our conversation and the time I spent with him. I'm going to take it slow. Besides, I need to focus on our opening, not think about the sexy man I want in my bed."

"You do have it bad."

She prances into the kitchen. "Did you find the pregnancy test?"

"Honestly, I was so tired I forgot all about it." I yawn, stretching.

Sofia gets down on her hands and knees and looks under the table. "That's odd. I don't see it."

"It's late. I'll worry about it tomorrow."

7 EVER

"You look like shit." Luca hands me a mug of black coffee.

"I couldn't sleep." I tossed and turned all night, thinking about the possibility of Noa carrying my baby. It changes everything because I can't have a child in the world I live in. It's too dangerous. The possibility of a kid has never entered my mind. I can't be a father. It's the worst thing that could happen, and yet, I find myself envisioning the spitting image of Noa in a child's face, and my heart raced all night long.

"Are you worried about being seen at the opening today?"

"No. I'm looking forward to it."

"According to the local news, it's the talk of the town. They've even closed down the main street and placed tables and chairs on the sidewalks to accommodate the amount of people that are expected to be there."

"Great. It will make it easier for me to blend in with the crowd."

"Where do you want me, sir?"

"Take the day off. I've got it handled."

"I have to admit, I was pretty envious of Noa and her father fishing yesterday."

"Go, have fun. I'll have our chef plan for fresh fish on the grill tonight."

"Your disguise is in a bag hanging amongst your wardrobe."

"Got it," I say, lifting my mug in the air and hitting the steps to my cabin. Unzipping the hanging bag, I find a dark brown, wavy, shoulder-length wig with a short beard and mustache. A pair of faded jeans with a hole in one knee and a T-shirt touting graphics of ABBA.

"Very funny, Luca." I chuckle. I'm more of a Led Zeppelin type of guy. I reach the bottom and pull out a pair of shoes. "Vans. Really, Luca?" I yell over my shoulder. "She certainly won't recognize me. I'd never wear any of this crap. Only for you, Noa. Only for you," I huff and change into my disguise and stand in front of the mirror. "This surely works. I don't recognize myself." The song "Dancing Queen" swims inside my head, and I have to shake it off. "I swear if that song gets stuck in my brain today, I'm going to kick Luca's ass."

I tug on a navy-colored hat and dark sunglasses to finish off my disguise and drive into town, parking in a roped-off area a few blocks from downtown. The streets are already buzzing with people. Outside of The Fork and Spoon is a chalkboard display listing the pizza pie of the day, along with freshly made lemonade with real fruit. The line is wrapped around the corner, and the scent of Italian herbs floats outside. Peering through the large pane widow with their logo printed on it, I see Sofia behind the counter, along with the man that had his hands on my woman. No sign of Noa. I move to the side to let people by me, and a colorful ice cream shop catches my eye a few doors down. It reminds me of one my mother and I used to frequent in Florida, and my mouth waters for a taste of its sugary goodness.

I step in line behind a mom and her pigtailed

daughter, who is as cute as they come. She has a bridge of freckles dancing on her nose.

She stands on her tiptoes, and her pigtails swish across her back as she gazes, mesmerized by the vibrant colors of sherbet.

"I don't know why you bother to look. You end up with the same thing every time," the mother says sweetly to the girl. "I'm so sorry," she turns and says to me.

"I'm not in any hurry."

Her mother prompts her with a throat clearing. The little girl's breath fogs up the glass, and she moves further toward the ice creams.

"I'll have that one." The little girl points.

"Bubblegum wins out again." Her mother laughs and lovingly twists the ends of one of her pigtails.

"Can I have a double scoop?" she asks, batting her eyes at her mother, who in turn looks inside her wallet.

"I'm afraid I only have enough for a single."

"Allow me." I step up to the register. "Get both of them whatever they'd like."

"You don't have to do that," the mother protests.

"I want to. It wasn't that long ago my mother was in the same position. Let me honor my mother by paying for it."

"Thank you for your kindness." She looks down at the girl. "Tell the kind man thank you."

She shyly tucks her chin and glances at me. "Thank you."

"You're very welcome." I step back behind them, and when the mother reaches for the cone, I stuff a couple of one-hundred-dollar bills in the pocket of her purse.

"Thanks again," the woman says, leading her daughter to a table.

"What can I get you?" the young teenage boy behind the counter asks me.

"I'll have a waffle cone with two scoops of vanilla ice cream with fresh strawberries, and chocolate drizzled on the top." It was my mother's favorite. As I wait for it to be prepared, I struggle to get napkins out of the dispenser, recalling my mother always took more than we needed because she knew I was going to be a mess. The simple memory of her makes me smile.

"Here you go, enjoy," the teen boy says, handing it to me over the glass encasement of ice creams.

I toss a couple of bucks in his tip cup, and the bell above the door jingles when I step outside and lick the cone before the ice cream drips on my hand.

"I'm glad to see people buying ice cream today. I

was hoping our grand opening would help the small businesses, not hurt them."

I turn to the voice, and I'm face to face with Noa. I press my lips together, trying to dislodge the lump in my throat.

She squints. "Do I know you? Nice shirt, by the way. Dancing Queen is one of my all-time favorite songs."

How did I not know such a tragedy about the woman I love? "Yeah, mine too," I say, deepening my voice. "I'm on vacation, enjoying the town."

"Well, it's your lucky day. My sister and I just opened Essex's first pizza parlor. We're giving away samples if you're interested."

"I'll check it out," I respond casually.

Her face lights up, and my heart aches. "Alright. Enjoy your visit and your ice cream. And I truly love the T-shirt." She points.

She spins on her flats, and it's all I can do not to grab her hips from behind and pull her close to me. I want to wrap my hand around her braid and tell her she's mine. She stops and speaks with a couple sitting at a table, and I can't help but stare. Her skin is sun-kissed, and she's damn beautiful. She's all I want.

Noa disappears inside the restaurant doors for a

moment and comes back with a craft full of lemonade, filling glasses for three children sitting with what appears to be their grandparents. She squats, talking to one of them, and her face is lit up like I've never seen it, yet there's still that hint of sadness lingering in the corners of her eyes. *That sadness has a name, and it's mine.* I want more than anything to erase those lines.

I eat my ice cream and find a shady spot underneath a tree in the park where I can see her come and go, serving people on the outside. Every now and then, Sofia comes out carrying a large silver platter filled with different slices of pizza. The samples are going quickly, but so are the white boxes being toted out the door by customers. I'd say they are a big success, and I'm so proud of both of them.

The day turns into evening, and the crowd finally starts to dwindle down. The streetlights pop on when Noa saunters out the front door, wiping her hands on an apron. Her gaze falls on me, and then she walks back inside, only to appear a few minutes later, carrying one of their to-go boxes.

"You never got a sample." She sways her hips towards me.

I stay still, not meeting her on my feet.

She eases down next to me and places the box in front of me. "You're missing out." She smiles, and my jeans become uncomfortable.

I move to open the box, but she stops me, touching the back of my hand. It feels so damn good.

"You've waited this long. Why don't you take it home and save it for later? I mean, by the size of the ice cream you scoffed down, you're probably still full," she teases, and it damn near does me in.

"I'll do that. I'll save it for later, but from the looks of things, your restaurant is a hit."

"I had no doubt that it would be. My sister is an amazing businesswoman."

"You're partners. You should take some credit too."

She stands. "My love for food and money is about all I had to contribute. Enjoy your pizza, Mr. ABBA man." She laughs with her head back, and as she walks away, I hear her singing "Dancing Queen."

Despite the awful song, I ache for her. Inhaling, I get up and take the box with me and find my car, driving back to the marina and ripping off the wig and beard combo, kicking out of my shoes. I go to tug off my shirt and stare down at the logo. "She loves ABBA," I mutter, opting to leave it on for now.

Picking up the intercom, I call the chef. "Has Luca returned with the fish?"

"No. He said he was having a great time and wanted to do some night fishing. He apologized and asked that I wait to find out what you wanted for dinner."

"I brought home a pizza. No need to cook. You can take the rest of the evening off," I tell him as I pour a glass of bourbon over an ice ball.

I've had many hard days in my life, but today was one of the most difficult. To see Noa and not be able to touch her damn near killed me, not to mention the number it did on my cock. I'll be hard for days.

Walking out onto the deck, I down my drink, watching fishermen coming back from their day's journey as nightfall sets in, and the only thing lighting the sky are the stars and the moon.

Settling inside, I take out a plate and open the pizza box. There's a note taped inside. Ripping the tape with my finger, I unfold the paper.

DID *you really think I wouldn't recognize the man I love regardless of what you were wearing?*

. . .

"FUCK," I grunt.

I hear the glass door to the boat slide open. "The shirt was a dead giveaway." Noa strolls inside. "I mean, I wasn't lying. They are my favorite group from the seventies, but you…" She waves a finger. "Too upbeat for your mood."

"How did you know where to find me?" I'm stunned she's standing in front of me, so close I can feel the heat radiating from her body.

"I felt you watching me, and I knew it was only a matter of time before you had to be close to me." She brushes a piece of hair off my forehead. "I do like this scruffier look you have going on." She presses her lips together, then her tongue sweeps over them, and I lose all self-control.

My hands fly in her hair, and I crash my mouth to hers, plunging my tongue inside with a violent kiss, working her lips apart. Her hands are in my hair, tightly gripping strands of it with the same force I'm giving her, pulling me closer. Her wanting sounds vibrate deep within her chest with desire, and it drives me mad.

Tempering the kiss further, our tongues tangle with a promise of what's to come. "Are you as hungry as I am?" I breathe against her lips.

"More." She places her hand in the middle of my chest and moves me backward until my ass is against the breakfast bar.

Turning only long enough to toss the pizza box on the floor, I spin back around and snag her hips and lift her up, setting her on the bar.

"I wish I could make your clothes dissolve." Her voice is all breathy. "At least the pants." Her gaze dips downward.

Placing my hands on either side of her face, she tilts her head to the side, inviting me to slide my lips down the column of her gorgeous, edible neck, and I oblige her. "God, I've missed you."

"You've wrecked me," she pants.

"I got your text." I chuckle next to her ear. As I move down her body, her skin has a sheen of sweat on it. She shoves the soft material of her dress down her arms, exposing a pale blue, lacy, low-cut bra, and my warm mouth can't resist.

She hisses, "Don't stop."

"I couldn't, even if I wanted to," I moan, and clasp her hips, kissing my way to her smooth stomach, dragging her dress down her sexy legs, leaving her in a thong. "I love these, but even this thin piece of material is in my way." I rip them off, and she gasps. I apply pressure between her legs, and she reacts by rocking her hips back and forth, moving in a mind-blowing rhythm. She leans back, and my tongue slides inside her ready-and-waiting folds, lapping her up until she's breathing in rapid pants, and then shudders.

"Yes!" she cries, and I don't stop until her breathing calms.

I stand tall, peering into her molten, dark eyes, with perspiration on her upper lip and strands of fallen hair around her face with damp unruliness. Her sexy look makes me drunker than any bourbon I could drink.

She leans forward, ripping my shirt over my head. Her nails dig into my chest, frantic to touch me, drawing blood to the surface, then her fingers frantically unbutton my jeans. I shove them and my boxers below my ass and drag her hips to mine, entering her in one move. I may have set the tone, but she starts the grueling pace that neither one of us can halt. It takes over, and we become one, grappling for each other's greatest pleasure. I'm lost in the feel of her wrapped around my dick. I have no functioning brain cells in this moment, only an animalistic duty to consume her over and over again until neither of us can walk.

Thrusting harder and harder, I hit the spot that

makes her seize up, drawing me deeper until her eyes roll back, and she nearly loses consciousness. I trap her against my chest, holding her tight and letting go with her.

8 NOA

He leaves me naked, picks me up, carries me to the plush off-white couch, and strips out of his jeans.

"What if someone walks in on us?" I speak with a dry mouth, thirsting for more already.

"You weren't too worried about that a moment ago." He chuckles, planting his lips around my taut nipple. "They all have the night off. The only one we have to worry about is Luca returning from fishing."

"Luca is here too?" He nods and plucks my nipple from his mouth, causing a sting of pain, but in a good way. "The two of you were on the dock yesterday, weren't you?"

"Damn, woman. You have Spidey-Sense running through your veins."

"I could feel your presence." I tilt his face to look into my eyes. "I'm sorry I told you I never wanted to see you again. I didn't mean it. And, for scratching you." She kisses the marks.

"Don't ever be sorry for clawing me in the heat of passion. You can mark me anytime." He exhales. "We both walked out for the same reason. All I want to do is protect you." He slides his hand to my abdomen and then abruptly sits. "Do you have something you want to share with me?"

I squint, not sure what he's referring to. "I missed you." My voice rises a few octaves with each word, guessing that's what he wants to hear.

He gets up, and I gain the pleasure of watching his backside as he walks over to a drawer and opens it, and then struts back with something gripped in his hand. "Is this for you or Sofia?" He tosses me the pregnancy kit.

I abruptly stand. "You were in my house!" I scramble for my dress, but he snatches me by the hand.

"I wanted to make sure you were okay."

"And you needed to break into my home to find out? You could have called me, or here's a thought, answered my text," I snap haughtily.

"Luca has my phone, and I only found out about your text yesterday when I arrived."

He lets go of my hand, and I wrestle with my dress to get into it. "It's a bit stalkerish, don't you think?"

He eases his way over to me with his hands outstretched. "I'm sorry. I didn't know any other way."

The look on his face is so sincere it melts my resolve to be angry, and I'm thankful he's here.

"You didn't answer my question?" He picks up the box and waves it at me.

"It's Sofia's," I lie, sort of. She did buy it.

He narrows one eye and raises the other brow. "Noa." He deepens his voice.

"Fine! I only partially lied. She bought it for me." I fold my arms over my chest, and he tugs on his boxers and jeans.

"It's unopened."

"Yes." I glare at him.

He grips my hand and drags me down the stairs. "Where are we going?"

"There's no time like the present."

I jerk free of him. "I'm not doing this now. Besides, you just spilled inside of me. It won't be accurate."

"Damn it!" He runs his hands through his thick hair. "I didn't use a condom. You get me so worked up I lose my mind." He grinds his teeth.

"That's not necessarily a bad thing," I try to tease, but he's not having it.

"I can't be a father!" he blares, and I falter backward. He tangles both of his hands in his hair and pulls. "Not a Leone." His voice is full of anguish, and it's heartbreaking.

"Hey." I approach him with caution, touching his forearm. "You're not a Leone."

"You don't fucking get it!" His eyes are filled with tears. "It's damn near impossible to escape who I am! If you're carrying my child"—he clutches his chest as if he's in agony—"you'll have to disappear from my life forever." He goes to his knees with his head hanging down and his shoulders bobbing as he sobs.

My heart wrenches seeing such a powerful man hurting so badly. I kneel in front of him and tip his chin upward, but he won't look me in the eye. "Look at me," I whisper tenderly.

His lashes bat a few times before he directs his gaze into my eyes. "I'm not your mother, and you're definitely not your father. If I am pregnant, I'm not going anywhere. I trust you to find a way out."

"You don't understand. Even with my father

behind bars, he'll find a way to destroy my life. In the end, he'll still control me."

"Then we'll disappear together."

His hand shakes, lifting it to place it on my belly. "I've never fathomed being a father before."

"We don't know if I am or not. We need to figure out a way for you to be free. Knowing if there is a little one growing inside of me can wait a few more days." I plant a kiss on his forehead. "Right now, all I want to do is love you." I slide my fingertips over his heart. "Can you do that?"

"Yes," he sniffs and stands, dragging me to his cabin, where we spend the rest of the night making love and clinging to one another.

"THE SUN IS ALREADY STARTING to rise," I purr against his chest. "I really need to get home before Sofia sends the cops out looking for me."

"You can't tell her or anyone that I'm here." He lightly runs his finger down my bare spine.

"I know. I'll make up some excuse. I'll tell her I had a one-night stand with a hot guy. It will thrill her."

His palm lands hard on my backside, and I yelp. "I'll be the only man touching you."

I crawl to my knees and straddle him. "Then I need sex more than every three months." I nip his nose with my teeth.

"Believe me, if I could be in your bed every night, I'd be a happy man. And I hope one day that happens. For now, we'll have to steal moments where we can."

I roll off the bed and walk into the bathroom to clean up and pull on my dress while he watches me with a sexy grin. "Have you devised a plan yet?"

He sits on the edge of the bed and then walks up behind me, both of us facing the mirror. "I have, and I pray like hell it works, but unless I can take down the entire organization, you'll always be at risk." He presses his lips to my shoulder.

"Where will it leave you?"

"Prison, dead, a free man, it's a crapshoot."

"Two out of three of those sound horrible." I turn in his arms, wrapping my arms around his waist.

"I don't have a choice. If I do nothing, I lose you, and that's not an option for me."

I prop my chin against the center of his chest. "I saw a picture of you with a redhead at a gala."

He cringes.

"I could tell you didn't want her on your arm by the look on your face."

"Could you now?" He clasps my ass with both of his hands.

"You didn't look at her the way you do me."

"As long as we're making admissions, Luca filmed you dancing with Ricco."

"I'm going to have a talk with him about invading my privacy," I snort.

"Good thing he did because I knew you didn't want him either. Please tell me Sofia did a background check on him."

"She did. I think he's a good guy, but I did overhear a conversation he was having with someone on the phone that raised a red flag for me."

"What did he say?" he scowls.

"He told whoever it was that 'he's not here, and there's been no sign of him,' then he added there was nothing to report."

"Shit!" He lets go of me. "He could be working for my father," he growls, storming into the bedroom and starts pacing.

"You think so? He seems so nice, and Sofia really likes him."

"Luca ran a background check, too, and hasn't come up with anything." He stops his pacing and locks his hands on my shoulders. "I don't want you to spend any time alone with him. And make sure you don't slip and mention my name. I'll have him tailed."

"What about Sofia? Do you think she's in danger?"

"No. If he is employed by my father, as long as I'm not in the picture, she'll be safe. I've covered my tracks well, and he thinks I'm in California on business."

"I recognized you yesterday. Do you think Ricco could have too?"

"No. I never came in contact with him."

"Can you tell me your plan?"

"You're better off not knowing."

"When will I see you again?"

"I can't honestly say." He drags me flush with his body. "Only when I know it's safe."

"I hate this." I pout.

"I'm sorry you fell in love with a man like me. You deserve so much more."

"I don't regret it, and you're all I ever want. And there is nothing wrong with you. You've got a good heart."

"You bring it out in me." He kisses me deeply.

"I love you, Ever," I rasp with my forehead pressed to his.

"I love you more. When are you going to pee on the stick?"

"Tomorrow morning. That's when the directions say is the best time to take the test."

"Okay. Text my phone."

"So, Luca will find out before you," I snicker. "If you want to know the results, you'll have to see me again."

We walk hand in hand up the stairs onto the main deck. Luca's jaw nearly hits the floor when he sees me. "How?"

"She saw right through the disguise." Ever laughs.

"ABBA? Really, Luca?" I can't help but tease him.

"It's good to see you, Noa." He hugs me.

"Seems like you've been seeing a lot of me lately." I cock a brow at him.

His stare locks on Ever's.

"It's okay. I know your boss can have a bit of an attitude if you don't do as he's ordered." I playfully smack Ever on the cheek.

"You seem to be the only one to keep him in check." Luca smiles and opens his arms.

I kiss him on the cheek. "Thanks for looking out

for him…and me. I've got to go explain my whereabouts to my sister."

"Do you need a ride?"

"No, I drove myself, and that's no longer your job."

"Be careful. Make sure you're not followed," Ever walks me to the door. "I'll see you soon, I hope. Remember what I said about Ricco. I'll have Luca contact you when I find out more. Forget what I said about texting my phone. Banish the number altogether. I'm going to have Luca destroy the SIM card. I'll have him buy two burner phones so that the two of you can communicate. Don't come back to the boat. I don't want you to raise any suspicion."

"Alright. Please be safe and come back to me." Our lips lock in a tender moment.

9 NOA

As soon as I park in our driveway, the front door swings open, and I catch the wrath of Sofia. "I've been texting you. I was so worried thinking something had happened to you!" Her fingertips are gripping her hips.

"I'm sorry." I meet her on the porch.

"You've got some explaining to do. Where the hell have you been?"

"When did you become my mother? I'm a grown woman, and if I want to stay out all night, I don't need your permission." I know I'm being a bitch, and she's only concerned for my safety, but she's being a bit overwhelming.

She sighs, tossing one hand in the air. "No, I'm

not your mother, but you and I have been through a lot together, and I worry about you."

I ease back on my irritation and fold my arms over her shoulders. "I'm sorry. I had a few too many glasses of wine while I was serving and went home with a stranger." *He was dressed as a stranger.*

"So, I've been up half the night worrying, and you've been having sex?" Her brows knit together.

I shrug and half grin.

She bursts out in laughter. "Good for you. Finally getting Ever out of your system."

Far from it. He is more a part of me than I thought possible.

"Wait." She holds me at arm's length. "You were drinking wine?"

"Yes, is that crime?"

She stares at my stomach. "What if you're…"

I cover her mouth with my hand. "Don't say it." I drop it and walk past her through the front door.

"I stopped at the drugstore on the way home last night and bought you another pregnancy test."

"Please stop. Can we talk about something else, like how well the grand opening did last night?" I sink to the couch, and my head whips around when I hear footsteps behind me.

Ricco stands awkwardly in the hallway. "I'm um…"

I swing my gaze to Sofia. "I thought you said you were up worrying about me all night?"

"Most of the night." She scrunches her nose as one shoulder lifts.

"She was concerned about you." Ricco steps into the living area. "Are you okay?"

My mind races to Ever's words about his thoughts on Ricco. "I'm fine. Ain't a girl allowed to have a little fun every now and then?"

"That's good to hear. Sofia told me about your ordeal in New York."

I glare so hard at Sofia that I'm sure bullets are darting from my eyes. "I asked you not to tell anyone."

She opens her mouth to say something, and he interrupts her. "I won't mention it to anyone. You have my word."

How good is his word? If he's working for the Leones, he's a danger to both of us. If he thinks I'm suspicious of him, the danger will be more imminent. "Thanks, I appreciate it."

He glances at his watch. "I should get going. I've got a lot of work to do before the restaurant opens in two hours."

Sofia walks him to the door and kisses his cheek. "I'll be there shortly," she says, shutting the door behind him.

"Whatever happened to taking things slow?"

"I couldn't help myself. He's so damn dreamy," she falls next to me.

I want to scold her, but I just accused her of not being my parent, and I recall feeling that same lure for Ever when I met him. There was no stopping what was evolving between us from the moment we met. "How much do you really know about him?"

"Ah, more than you knew about Ever." She rolls her eyes.

"We both need to be more careful," I relent. I have to admit, I've never seen her so happy.

"So, who was this stranger you had a hot night of sex with?"

"Someone passing through Essex on vacation."

"At least you won't have to bump into him in town."

I'd spend every night in his arms. "True."

"It's a start, right…I mean after Ever."

"After Ever," I repeat her words and get to my feet. "I'm going to take a long hot shower and a quick nap, then work a few hours on my blog. I'll be at the restaurant to help with the lunch crowd."

"Ricco and I can handle it until you get there," she shouts over her shoulder right before I close my bedroom door.

In the middle of my bed is the drugstore bag with the pregnancy test that Sofia purchased. "Not you again," I huff, peeling out of my clothes and hitting the warmth of the shower, letting it rain down my body. I can still feel him touching me. How is that possible? Drake never owned and commanded my body like Ever does. Part of me feels ashamed. Did Drake miss out on experiencing this sensation because he was married to me? Did he get a taste of it with Angelica? How do I know this inexplicable connection I have with Ever won't fade?

I lather my body and make circular motions over my belly. "It won't. I love him with every part of my being, and if you're growing inside of me, little one, I'll have a part of him forever, no matter what happens."

Drying off, I change into a pair of casual white shorts and a silky shimmery avocado green sleeveless top, and a pair of sandals and finish my current food blog, sending it out into the world, then type a few more words on my personal blog, picking up where I left off.

. . .

WAS it really the nail in my coffin, or just the beginning of a new story? I'd like to think anything is possible, even the impossible. Why should our lives be directed by a few defining moments unless it's to make us see the things we couldn't before, like what we thought love was.

Is it distinctive with one person? Or does it vary from person to person? We really don't truly know until you find that one someone who settles deep within your soul.

THE DOORBELL RINGING has me jumping to my feet. I tiptoe over the hardwood floor and peek through the blinds to see a delivery man at my doorstep.

Unlocking the deadbolt, I slowly open the door. "I have a package that needs to be signed for," the man says, handing me a clipboard.

"Thank you." I scribble my signature and give it back to him.

"Also, I'm to tell you there will be a company showing up at your place to install cameras."

"Oh, really." I smack my lips. "You can tell whoever is giving you orders," like I don't know who it is, "that I don't approve. I won't be monitored in my own home." I slam the door, locking it.

Grabbing a knife from the kitchen, I cut open the

tape, binding the box, and find a cell phone inside. "Luca works fast," I mumble, turning it on. A message pops up right away from Luca.

DON'T GIVE *out this number to anyone. If you need something, call me. And, yes, I knew you'd be angry about the security being installed.*

I TYPE QUICKLY.

TELL *him he does not have my permission to do so. I refuse.*

I STUFF it in my purse before he can respond and snag my car keys, and put the top down on my convertible, enjoying the warm weather. For a Sunday, the downtown area is already busy. There's a line forming outside the restaurant, and I see my dad outside carrying boxes of pizza.

"Hey, Papa. What are you doing?"

"Lending a hand," he says and gives the boxes to a

family waiting outside, stuffing cash in his palm. "*Grazie*," he tells them.

"I didn't know Sofia recruited you to help." I chuckle.

"Your madre kicked me out of the house and told me to go find something to do."

"That means you must have been driving her crazy," I snort. "Come on, I'll lend a hand." I drape my arm around his shoulder and walk with him into the restaurant.

Sofia is taking orders, and the chef is flipping dough in the air. Dad grabs another box and heads outside. I lay my purse in Sofia's office and nab a white apron off a hook.

"Where do you need me?" I ask Sofia as I twist my hair into a braid.

"Taking orders at the outside tables."

I stuff a pen in my apron and snatch a tablet for the orders. As soon as one table leaves, it's filled. The busboy is having a hard time keeping up, and I see Ricco assisting him. At one point, I sense Ever and look across the street to see a vehicle with deeply tinted windows, and I know he's behind them, watching me. My body warms out of my control, and there's a profound throbbing between my thighs. I can feel my cheeks grow pink with my need for him.

The window rolls down an inch or two, and a single finger bends over its side. I casually make the same motion back, and he rolls up the window. The car pulls onto the road, and I watch him drive off.

When I turn around to take an order inside, I see Ricco and my father off to the side talking. "I wonder what that's about?"

When the lunch crowd starts to thin, I corner my dad. "Hey. Thanks for helping out today."

"It was *divertimento*."

I laugh. "I'm glad you enjoyed it. I saw you earlier talking to Ricco. What do you think about him?"

"He seems nice enough."

"Were you discussing The Fork and Dough?"

"*Un pochino*." He pinches his fingers together. "He seemed more interested in my *figlie*."

"Daughters. You mean one specific daughter?"

"No. He was asking about you. Don't *preoccuparti*. I didn't tell him what you shared with me." He twists his fingers at his lips as if he's sealing them shut.

"I appreciate that." I wipe my hands on my apron. "What specifically was he asking you?"

"He said you no came home last night." He waves his hand and closes his eyes. "It's *non sono affari miei*."

Well, it's certainly none of Ricco's business.

"I told him I knew *niente*."

"Thanks, Papa." I squeeze his arm. "You tell Mama you were a lifesaver today." I storm inside with every intention of confronting Ricco, but he's working behind the counter shoulder to shoulder with Sofia. It worries me the way she's looking at him. She's fallen for him, and he may be just as evil as Carmine Leone. A wolf in sheep's clothing comes to mind. A text comes in from Ever, and I take a minute to respond and tuck the phone in the pocket of my apron.

Ricco finally leaves her side and heads to the storeroom, and I follow him. "Why were you asking my father about my whereabouts last night?" My tone is clipped when I shut the door, closing us inside.

"I, um…"

"Are you working for the Leone family?" I blurt out before I can stop myself and glare at him.

10 EVER

I'm leaving Essex more determined to break free from my family than I've ever felt before. I still don't know if she's carrying my baby or not, but I'm going to imagine that she is, so it will fuel the fire in me. "A baby," I whisper.

"What was that, sir?" Luca asks, looking at me in the rearview mirror.

I resorted to the back seat so that I could get a clear view of Noa while she worked. My heart pounded the moment she knew it was me behind the dark windows. "Did she get the package?"

"Yes, and she texted me a message."

"Let me guess." I chuckle. "She's pissed about the cameras."

"She refused them, sir."

"Stubborn woman," I huff, crawling into the front seat. "Find a way to get them installed anyway."

"She's going to make that very difficult."

"I trust that you'll convince her. I want eyes on her, especially if she's carrying…" I bite my tongue.

"Is she pregnant?"

"I don't know for sure. She wouldn't take the damn test."

"As much as I'd love to see you be a father…" He takes his eyes off the road, his face buried in concern.

"I know. Trust me, I know. How are we on time for the airport?"

"We'll make it, but barely. I hadn't planned on the pit stop."

"I had to lay my eyes on her one more time because I don't know if I'll see her again."

He flips his blinker on, turning onto the highway.

"Give me the phone." I extend the palm of my hand.

"It's in the glove box."

Pressing the button, I take my phone out and text her.

. . .

PLEASE DON'T FIGHT *me on the cameras. You know I'm only looking out for you.*

I wait for her response.

GO TO HELL, *and I'm mean that lovingly.*

I BURST OUT LAUGHING. "Yep, damn stubborn woman."

WHY CAN'T *you do as you're told? It would make things a lot easier.*

I GIVE IT A MINUTE, but she doesn't respond. "I've either pissed her off, or she got busy." I toss the phone back into the glove box. "Let me know what she responds."

"Great. You piss her off and leave me to pick up the crap." Luca chuckles. "Have you heard from your father?"

"No, not since he advised me not to purchase the property in California."

"Advised? That's a polite term," he grunts.

"My security team has had eyes on Victor. They reported he's been nosing around our fake addresses. He's going to be a problem."

"I agree."

My phone vibrates with my father's number. "His ears must have been ringing. Hello."

"When are you due back?"

"My flight lands at five."

"Did you walk on the deal?"

"Yes, thanks to your council." It kills me to say it.

"Victor has requested that he attend your meeting with the acting chief of police."

"I don't need nor want his help," I respond firmly, keeping my aggravation at bay.

"If you're sure you can handle the situation by yourself, I'll back him off."

"I'm positive I don't need Victor's type of help. I'll have Bentley bowing to you by the end of my meeting."

"Sounds like a confident man."

"I am. You've taught me well." Bile rises in my throat, knowing how true it is.

"Alright. I'll let you handle it on your own."

"Thank you for trusting me."

"You've earned it."

"I'll report to you tomorrow." I hang up. "Stop the car!" I bark.

Luca swerves to the side of the road, and I open the door, lean my hands on my knees and lose the contents of my breakfast on the asphalt. Standing tall, I inhale and wipe my mouth with my knuckles. "This has to work."

"I don't mean to rush you, sir, but you're going to miss your flight if you don't get back in the car."

Swallowing hard, I slide into the seat and roll the window down for fresh air to blow in my face, and Luca weaves back into traffic.

"Are you okay?"

"I will be once this is all over."

"There's a real possibility you may have to kill one of them before it ends, and this plan of yours could take a terrible turn."

"I'm well aware of both, but if I can't make it happen, I don't want to live anyway, not without Noa and my child. I can't take this life anymore."

11 NOA

"Are you going to continue to sputter, or are you going to answer me!"

Ricco bounces both of his hands out in front of him. "Keep your voice down."

"Don't tell me what to do," I snarl.

"It's not what you think."

"Then clear it up for me!" I'm in his face.

"I can't. It will only put you in more danger than you already are."

"What do you know about any of it?"

His jaw clenches, and his cheeks roll inward. "I don't work for Carmine Leone."

"If you don't spill what you know right now, I'm going to call the police." I grind my teeth.

"Fine, but you can't fill your sister in."

"Are you using her?" I narrow my eyes.

"No. I really do like her. It was you that I was using."

I falter backward. "You're using me to get close to Ever." The realization smacks me in the face.

"Yes."

I press my back against the door and cross my arms. "Elaborate."

"I work for the FBI."

"Prove it!" I bark.

"My badge is in my car."

"I'm never turning Ever into you."

"I'm not after him. I want his father. Unfortunately, they are tied together."

"I won't help you. Besides, I haven't seen him since I left New York. Things ended badly with us."

"Then why are you protecting him?"

"Because I don't want to see him pay for the sins of his father."

"Ever Christianson is not an innocent man. He's done things that could land him behind bars for the rest of his life."

"He was forced into their world."

"I believe you. It just doesn't make him innocent.

I've been investigating the Leones for several years. I know that Nick Leone is responsible for your husband's murder."

I feel like all the air is sucked out of my lungs. "Then why isn't he behind bars?"

He furrows his brows. "You knew he killed him."

"It's what ended things between Ever and I. Nick threatened to lay the blame on Ever."

"You left him to protect him from his family. This I can work with. I'm willing to offer Ever his freedom to provide me evidence of the things his family has done."

"Why would you do that, and why would I believe you?"

"I've read Ever's history. It's very tragic. Imagine being a young boy and finding the only parent you've ever known face down in a pool, then being hauled off by a monster. According to the reports I've read, he physically abused Ever for many years."

"He bears the scars on his back."

"It's not the outward scars that torment him. He locked him in a cage until Ever caved to him. He'd feed him breadcrumbs and water. I have pictures of him nearly starved to death."

Tears rain down my face. "Why didn't someone help him?"

"There's always been a bigger picture."

I march within inches of him and strike him across the cheek with an open hand. "You bastard! You're no better than his father!"

"I'd agree, but I wasn't the one on his case until a few years ago. The damage had already been done."

I walk in a circle, with my tears spilling down my shirt. "What else did he do to him?"

"Are you sure you want the details?"

"Yes, damn it!" Do I?

"When he turned fourteen, Carmine thought his boy should become a man, but Ever showed no interest. He hired two women to change his mind. They tied him down and…"

"Stop!" I cry, throwing my hand in the air.

"He landed in the hospital, and it wasn't the last time."

"Why didn't anyone help him?" I repeat, wailing in agony for him.

"They were using him. They knew he'd grow up and despise his father. He was their way to get to his family." He steps close to me. "There's more."

I cover my ears with my hands. "I don't want to hear any more."

"It's not about Ever. It's about me."

My head shakes with tears still streaming as I drop my hands.

"I'm Carmine Leone's bastard son. He has no idea I exist, and neither does Ever. When my mother was just a young girl, she got in some trouble, and her parents kicked her out of the house. She was living on the streets and surviving the only way she could. She was delivered to Carmine's room. She got pregnant."

I gasp.

"So, you see, I hate him as much as you do. If he would have known about me, my life could have easily been Ever's. That's why I want to help him. I've dedicated my adult life to taking down the Leone family."

"You really want to help him?"

"Yes. I need you to set up a meeting between me and Ever."

"I…I don't know."

"It's a lot to take in. Think about it. This may be Ever's only way out."

"Hey, what's going on in here?" Sofia asks, opening the door. Her gaze fixates on me then she glares at Ricco. "Did he hurt you?"

I sniff and dry my tears. "No, nothing like that."

"Why are you crying?"

I glance over my shoulder at Ricco. "You need to tell her the truth. This family has had enough secrets and lies. If you want my help, you'll explain everything to her."

"Whatever it is, it will have to wait until we're closed. There are already people waiting in line for the dinner rush."

Ricco hangs his head. "I'll tell her."

"Good. We'll talk after you do. I need to get out of here." I push past Sofia.

I run out the back door of the restaurant and straight into my car. I skid out of my parking spot and don't slow my speed until I'm parked at the marina. I sprint the length of the dock to the boat and frantically run up the steps, and burst through the glass doors.

"Where is he?" I ask, out of breath.

"Are you okay? Did someone hurt you?" Luca's eyes fill with fear, scanning my body.

"I need to talk to him."

"He's gone back to New York."

"Get him on the phone!" I shout.

"I can't. He's in flight, and he's asked me not to contact him until the end of the week."

"Why?"

"He's putting a plan in motion to take down his family, and he doesn't want to risk the contact."

I grab him by the shoulders. "I have a way out for him."

"How?"

"Ricco Bonetti is an FBI agent, and he's Carmine Leone's son."

"You didn't tell him anything, did you?"

"No."

"Stay right here," he orders and disappears, returning with a laptop. "I searched his name and came up with limited information. Did he say if Ricco is his real name?" He sits next to me and sets his laptop on the coffee table.

"I didn't think to ask him."

"Did he show you a badge?"

"He said it was in his car."

"So, you don't know if he was lying or not?"

"He knew things."

"What sort of things?"

Tears threaten to fall again. "Things that were done to Ever when he was younger. He knew Nick killed my husband."

His fingers fly over the keyboard.

"Did you know the horrible things his father did to him?" My lip trembles.

"No. He never spoke of them other than the scars on his back."

"He did unspeakable things to Ever."

"I don't doubt it." His eyes water.

"Carmine Leone needs to pay." I sit tall.

"Here it is. How did I miss this?" He points to the screen.

"How do you have access to FBI personnel?"

"I'm not allowed to tell you. According to this, Ricco Bonetti joined their force several years ago, about the time Ever turned twenty-five."

I scan the words on the screen. "He's older than Ever."

"Yes, by five years."

"He says his life's mission is to take down the Leone crime family, and he wants to help Ever."

"Ever has already put something in motion that can't be stopped. If it works, he won't need his help."

"And, if it doesn't?"

"God help him if he fails." He exhales a breath of sadness.

I get to my feet and stomp past him.

"Where are you going?"

"To New York."

He runs in front of me and prevents me from leaving. "I can't let you do that, Noa. They'll kill you the minute you land."

"I can wear a disguise."

"It won't work. The second you charter a plane, they'll know it."

"I have to help him," I plead.

"I feel the same way, but he's ordered me to stay out of it."

"Then talk to Ricco. Tell him everything you know about the Leones and Ever."

"I can't do that without talking to Ever first."

"Damn it, Luca! This could save his life!" I can tell he's mulling it over by the way he's chewing on the inside of his cheek.

"As much as I hate to admit it, perhaps you're right."

"I'll bring him by here tonight after the restaurant closes, along with my sister." I open the door.

"Promise me when you walk out that door, you won't get on a plane?"

"I promise. There's something I've been putting off I need to handle, and it may just be the persuasion that Ever needs." I dart out the door and drive like a bat out of hell to the cottage, bolting into my room and ripping open the package.

I pee on the stick, and my insides shake as I wait for the results. When it finally becomes apparent, I grab the burner phone and snap a picture, sending it to Luca along with a message.

SEND THIS TO EVER.

12 EVER

"Chief Bentley."

"Mr. Christianson." He greets me with a firm handshake in his office.

"Ever, please."

"Have a seat." He points to a chair across from his desk and closes his door, then sits, positioning himself in his seat. "What can I do for you?"

"I know you are just getting settled into this position, but I need to make you aware of what's been going on in this city with the Leone family."

"Ah, Carmichael mentioned the family name." He rocks back in his chair and tugs at his graying beard before he folds his hands in his lap.

"I have information on a business deal that will be going down involving military-grade explosives."

He chuckles. "And what do you want in return?"

"Freedom."

"I'm not following you."

"I'm one of Carmine Leone's sons."

"You're telling me you want to turn your family in for you to walk away with no repercussions?" He sits tall.

"Yes. Carmichael was bought and paid for by my father, so he looked the other way. I understand you are a man that stands behind your badge."

"When is this deal going down?"

"I meet with a man named Stanley Turro tomorrow. He's been wavering on the deal, and my father wants me to seal it and set up the exchange. I've compiled other evidence against my family." I open my briefcase and hand him a file.

He takes a minute, thumbing through it. "These are notes by you, not real evidence."

"My father keeps a log of everything he's ever done."

"Do you have access to it?"

"Not at this moment, but I will get my hands on it. The last page is the list of goods being sold to Mr. Turro."

"Damn. There has to be an even bigger fish than your father to get explosives like these."

"All I know is that it was someone high ranking in the military. His name will be listed in the journal entries, and you'll be able to take them all down."

"Why haven't you gone above Carmichael's head?"

"Because the judges in this town get a paycheck from my father."

"You're talking about taking down New York's government as well as your family." His eyes widen.

"Are you up to the task, Chief Bentley?"

He rests back in his chair. "You're a brave man coming here not knowing if I'm owned by your father or not."

"Are you?"

"No. I abhor men like Leone."

"Then do we have a deal?"

"I'm going to need to call in backup for this one. The FBI would be my choice."

"I'm sure they have plenty of files on my family. They've investigated us several times over the years but haven't been able to make anything stick."

"So why didn't you go to them?"

"Because they sat back and watched what he did to me for years and did nothing when I was a child."

"I have some agents I trust."

"This is only happening if you can ensure my freedom."

"You have my word." He extends his hand.

"I'm afraid I'll need it in writing."

"You'll have it. Contact me when you have a time and date. I advise you to find your father's journal in the meantime."

"It's my first priority as soon as I leave your office." I stand. "My family will kill me if they get wind of our conversation, and in all likelihood, one of my father's strong arms will follow up with you on our conversation. My goal today was to pay you off."

"If someone shows up, I'll reassure them that I'm now employed by the Leone family."

"We'll be in touch." Picking up my briefcase, I casually march out of his office, keeping aware of my surroundings. As soon as I step outside, I put my sunglasses on and scan the area. Victor is parallel-parked across the street, watching me. Yanking open the door, I climb behind the wheel and ease into traffic. Out of the side-view mirror, I see Victor get out and cross the street. "He didn't waste any time," I mumble. My gut tells me to trust Bentley, but in actuality, there are only two people I trust: Noa and Luca.

I park outside my father's building and take the elevator to the third floor and smile at his secretary as I move past her. His door is open, and he's standing at the window, looking out.

"You gotta minute?" I tap on his door.

He twists his neck to look over his shoulder. "I've been waiting for you."

I join him at the window. "It's done. Bentley will fall in line where Carmichael left off."

He angles toward me, clasping my shoulder. "Good job. I knew I sent the right man to do the work."

"You can plan on tomorrow going just as well with Turro. I'll have the goods moved by the end of the week."

"They'll be a rather large bonus in it for you."

"It's not about the money. It's about securing our families' organization." I literally vomit in my mouth, and I can't wait for this to be finally over.

"What's going on in here?" Nick pops his head in the door.

"Your brother has secured the chief of police for us," he says with pride.

"Nice job, man." Nick slaps me on the back.

"I've got a conference call with a potential client." Our father moves us toward the door.

"You have time for lunch?" I ask Nick.

"I do, in fact. I had to reschedule my meeting. Too bad The Italian Oven isn't still in operation. There's no other Italian food in Manhattan that can compare to it."

"Perhaps we should have considered keeping it open rather than selling the property." I chuckle, hating my words.

"Unless we could have kept the hot little number running it, the food wouldn't have been the same. Those sisters took off with their tails between their crotches and never looked back. I told you that woman was using you," he says as the elevator door closes us in.

In my mind, this is where I beat the crap out of him. Instead, I tuck my hands in the pockets of my slacks and nod in agreement while swallowing the acid churning up from my stomach.

We walk a few blocks down to a Chinese restaurant that's serving a buffet luncheon. After we fill our plates, we find a seat positioned in the front window. I jump right into conversation.

"I've been contemplating our current security at the office building. We've had multiple scares of investigations, and so far, we've been able to keep them out of the building. With our organization expanding into…let's say, more expensive goods, I feel anything that might expose the truth, we should have cleared from the offices."

He rakes the fork across his teeth and smacks his lips. "You mean like our father's journal."

"Precisely."

"You don't have to worry about that. It's already been taken care of."

"Is it in a secure location that the FBI or our father's enemies can't access?" I take a bite of my egg roll.

"I don't think they are going to raid a locker at the subway station. He listed it under another name that has no connection to our family."

"Brilliant." I can't blatantly ask for the name, so I'll have to follow my father when he uses the subway. He has to update it periodically. "You know they have cameras at the stations."

He grins. "Don't worry. The employee that maintains the video is one of our men."

Of course it is. "Alright, then I can take it off my list of things we need to secure."

"You've changed," he states, wiping the corner of his mouth.

"I wasn't given a choice."

"I'm glad you survived all the hell our father put

you through. I can say I was always happy I wasn't on the receiving end of his wrath."

No, he'd stand by and watch, saying nothing. I begged him to free me from that damn cage in the basement of our home. "It's all in the past."

"Good, I'm glad we're finally brothers." He dips his fork into his fried rice.

A brother I want to see behind bars for the rest of his life. "Me too."

Victor meanders in and sits next to Nick, snarling his lip. "Seems you were successful with Bentley."

"Checking up on my work? When did that become part of your job description?" I spat.

"He's right. You need back the hell off," Nick chimes in, glaring at Victor.

"I don't trust him, and neither should you. Men like us don't do an about-face like he's claiming to have done."

"Shut up, Victor," Nick warns.

I toss my napkin on my plate. "Perhaps it's time you find another job. With me fully on board, we don't need you anymore."

"You're not going to do that. I know where the bodies are buried." He slouches, draping an arm on the back of Nick's chair.

"You mean the ones you've disposed of." I smirk.

He straightens his spine and shoves his finger in my face. "Don't fucking try me, pretty boy. I'll nail your coffin shut."

"That's enough! You need to leave." Nick shoves him, and all eyes turn on us.

Victor stands, adjusting his suit jacket. "Nothing to see here, people." He sneers, then turns to me. "I'm watching you," he says in a lower voice before he walks away.

I glower at Nick.

"I'll handle Victor. You keep up the good work you're doing."

"If you don't deal with him, I will," I threaten, hoping like hell it doesn't come to that.

He laughs. "I really do like this side of you, brother."

"We're family. We stick together." That couldn't be further from the truth. The bill comes, and I pick it up before Nick does. "I got this."

"We need to do this more often without the old man."

"I'll put it on my calendar for every Monday."

"I'll have my secretary fill mine in. Now that you're committed to this family, you should really think about hiring you some smoking hot secretary. It will help take your mind off that tight-ass filly."

"Noa?" I ask as if I don't know who he's talking about.

"That would be the one."

"She's long forgotten, brother. I used her for what I needed, nothing more." *I'll never forget her. She's all I think about.*

We walk back to the office, and I kill the rest of the day doing paperwork, waiting for my father to leave. Finally, at six, he sticks his head in my office.

"You're still here?"

"Yes. I'm working on some future acquisitions for us."

"Don't get so caught up on this place you forget to enjoy some of the finer things in life, son."

"You mean women," I scoff.

"There isn't anything better than a sexy woman in your bed." He lifts his wrist to look at his watch. "In fact, one is being delivered to my house as we speak. I have a pit stop to make, and I don't want to leave her waiting too long."

"Get out of here, then." My grin is in place, but my stomach is revolting.

"Let me know as soon as Turro has signed the

deal." He taps his hand on the doorframe, and I wait to hear the ping of the elevator arriving.

Bolting from my seat, I take off down the stairs and peek through the small window in the door for the elevator to open and my father to walk out. He's gripping his suitcase in one hand, the other is in his pocket, and he's whistling a tune.

I follow far enough behind him that he can't make out my footsteps in the crowd of people making their way in the same direction. It's the busiest time of day for the subway station, which means no one will be paying him any attention. He flashes his prepaid badge on the scanner, and I dig out change from my pocket, tossing it in the metal bin when he's cleared the gated area.

I duck behind a column when he stops at a locker. He digs the key from his pocket and unlocks it. His face is shielded by the locker door, but I can see the cover of the journal underneath the door as he makes notes in it. Five minutes have passed before he places it back inside and shuts it. I stay out of sight, waiting for the subway train to arrive. Once he's on board and it's cleared the station, I make my way to the locker and jimmy it open, tucking the journal inside my suit jacket. "Got you," I stammer, feeling victorious.

13 NOA

The past twenty-four hours have been pure hell. I can't stop thinking about Ever.

What's he going through?

Is he being careful?

Or is he even still alive?

"Gah." I pace the deck. "I wish you would just reach out to him," I grumble at Luca.

"I'm in agreement with Luca. We need to let this play out," Ricco states, leaning against the railing.

"Then it's two against two," Sofia says, glaring at Ricco.

She was utterly pissed when she found out he was an FBI agent and initially tried to use me. I'm not sure she'll forgive him. As much as I dislike what he did, he was doing his job, and I want to believe he's truly trying to help Ever.

"Here's an idea." I change my path, walking toward Ricco. "Why don't you go to New York?"

"I can't."

"Can't or won't?" Sofia taps the toe of her shoe on the ground.

"I've been ordered to stand down until further notice."

"You're going to stand by and watch, just like they did when he was a child, and not help him." I grind my teeth.

"Regardless of what you think of me, I would've never let them abuse him."

"How is now any different?" Sofia snaps.

She cried her eyes out when Ricco told her the details of Ever's abuse. Luca had to leave the room to compose his emotions. He lays blame on himself for not seeing it. He didn't step into Ever's realm until the brunt of it was over. I tried to console him, but he said he'd never forgive himself.

"This is Ever's choice…his plan. It may work."

"Chances are it won't." Luca steps up. "His father's connections are way deeper than any of us know. Yes, there are clients of his that would love nothing more than to see Carmine Leone on his knees, but they are terrified of him for good reason. If one of them clues him in on what Ever is planning, he will take his own son's life."

"If anyone is to blame, Luca, it's me."

"How do you figure?"

"He's doing all of this for me. If I hadn't walked into his life, he'd be safe."

"That's not true. Ever wanted out. You were just his motivator," he cups my cheek. "He'd do anything for you."

"The waiting around, waiting to hear anything, is gnawing at my insides."

"You've got to find a way to settle down for the baby's sake," Sofia says.

"You're pregnant?" Ricco pushes off the railing.

"Yes." I exhale.

"Does Ever know?"

I switch my gaze to Luca, and he bites his lower lip. "Luca?" I already know the answer by the look on his face.

"I couldn't send it to him. I was afraid it would distract him from focusing on his plan."

My head hangs between my shoulders in despair. "He doesn't know." I breathe.

"Look at me." Sofia marches over and snags my face between her hands. "You and Ever are going to be together to raise this baby and have many more."

My lip quivers. "I wish I knew that for sure. Life hasn't exactly turned out like I planned it."

"What would Papa tell you?" She stares me in the eyes.

"*Prepara limonata*," I say begrudgingly.

"That's right. Make lemonade. For the next couple of days, you need to stay busy to help keep your mind off of Ever every single minute. I'm going to call and get you in with a midwife I know. She'll fit you in. You need to make sure you and your baby are alright. If you're three months along, she could probably even tell you the sex of the baby."

I rub my belly. "You're right. I should make sure the baby is okay."

"I'll call her now and see if she can work you in sometime this week."

"Will you go with me?"

"Go, I'll cover the restaurant," Rico offers.

"Are you still working for me?" Sofia scowls.

"Until I'm ordered to go somewhere else."

"Did you really manage a restaurant?" She's back to being snippy with him.

"Actually, I did. I worked my way through college learning the ropes, and I managed a restaurant for one year before I was picked up into the FBI training program."

"At least that's one thing you didn't lie about." Her eyes roll.

He walks over to her and peers into her eyes. "I didn't lie about my feelings for you. They are genuine, and when this is all over with, I intend on proving it to you if you'll allow me."

She shrugs him off, taking my hand. "We'll see."

"Sofia," I scold her quietly. "I really don't think he's a bad guy."

"He's not, and I have every intention of letting him grovel. Think how great the makeup sex will be." She winks at me.

At times I wish I was more like her. She seems to find the good in things more than I do.

We load into her car, and she calls her friend. "You're in luck, she had a last-minute cancellation, and we can head over right now."

"Wow, I wasn't expecting it to be today. I don't know if I want to do this without Ever."

"Please don't back out. You don't have to find out the sex. She can write it down and put it in an envelope, and the two of you can open it when he comes back."

"If he comes back," I whisper out the window so she can't hear me.

She takes my hand, and we walk into the small office together. There's only one other person in the waiting room with a child bouncing on her knee. The receptionist hands me the paperwork, and I nervously fill it out. Sofia takes the clipboard from me and gives it back to the front desk, and within a matter of minutes, my name is being called.

"Noa Sutton."

I stay frozen in my chair, and Sofia stands with her hand extended. "Come on. It's going to be okay."

I nod, and my sweaty palm meets hers. We walk in together.

"Please step on the scale." The medical assistant, wearing navy blue, points. She scribbles down the number. "From the information you given us, it doesn't appear that you've gained any weight. In fact, you've lost two pounds."

"Is that normal?" I ask.

"It can be if you've had some nausea."

"She hasn't been eating much," Sofia tells her.

"Here's a restroom. I'm going to need a urine sample to confirm that you are pregnant." She hands me a container with a lid. "You can just leave it on the sink. I'll get it when you're done."

I do as she asks, then return to Sofia's side, who is my lifeline at the moment.

"The midwife will address any questions that you have." She drops the clipboard to her side and ushers us into a room, and takes my vitals. "You'll need to change into this lovely paper gown for your exam," she pulls one out of a drawer. "Jackie will be in to see you in a few minutes," she states, closing the door to the room that at this moment seems suffocatingly small.

"I don't feel so good," I swallow hard, removing my clothes and replacing them with the thin blue gown.

"You're going to be just fine." Sofia sits beside me, patting my hand.

As promised, a few minutes later, the midwife opens the door and says hi to Sofia, and introduces herself to me. "Hi, Noa. My name is Jackie, and I'm going to take good care of you and your baby."

"Hello," is the only response I have to give.

"If it's alright with you, I'd like to ask you a few questions while I examine you." She pats the table, covered with white paper.

"I'm not going anywhere." Sofia gives me a nudge.

I step up and sit on the table.

Jackie does a basic exam first, starting with my ears, eyes, and throat. "Lay back, and scooch so that your butt is on the edge." She folds down the stirrups and walks to the side of me. "I'm going to do a breast exam if that's alright."

"Okay."

"It says in your chart your last period was three months ago."

"Yes."

"Did you suspect you were pregnant earlier?"

"No. My periods have been irregular since the day they started. It isn't unusual for me to skip one or two."

"Fair enough," she says and moves to my feet. "Your urine test did confirm that you are pregnant, so I'm going to do a pelvic exam and then a sonogram."

I nod and bite my bottom lip through the exam.

"So far, so good," she says, snapping off her gloves and tossing them in the trash. "I'll have my portable sonogram brought into the room. You can sit up," she says, dropping the stirrups.

A few minutes later, a machine is rolled into the room, and a technician sets it up. "My name is Vivian, and I'll be performing your sonogram. If you'll lie back, I'll extend the table to make you more comfortable." She smiles. "Would you like a warm blanket?"

"No, I'm good."

She angles the head of the table so that I'm not lying flat. Taking a sheet from a cabinet, she covers my lower body and exposes my belly. She squeezes a gel on the end of the probe. "I've warmed it, so it shouldn't be too cold." Rolling it around my belly, she takes some measurements. "Do you want to hear the heartbeat?"

I nod, and Sofia is on her feet, staring at the screen. I hold my breath, waiting, and then I hear the faint fast sound, and she turns up the volume. "There it is," she says sweetly.

"It's so fast," I gasp.

"Healthy babies always have much faster heart rates than adults."

Jackie knocks, coming into the room. "How do things look?" she stands behind Vivian.

"Very normal. By all the measurements, she's thirteen weeks along, and in this view, though rare at this gestational age, I could tell you the sex if you'd like."

"No," I snap, harsher than I mean to. "I'm sorry. I want to wait and find out with the baby's father."

"No problem. I can seal the information in an

envelope for you."

"Thank you."

"I'm a little concerned that you've lost a couple of pounds. You need to try and increase proteins and eat small, frequent meals. Other than that, everything looks perfect. Do you have any questions for me?"

Is the father of my child going to meet him or her? Does he want a child? What do I do if he doesn't survive? How will I raise this baby alone? "No," I finally reply.

"I think she's in shock. She'll have questions later, and I'll have her write them down. Thank you so much for fitting her into your schedule," Sofia tells her.

"No problem at all. You'll need to see me once a month until your eight-month mark. I'll do another sonogram at that time. If you have any concerns, please call my office. If you have any bleeding, go to the emergency room, and they will page me. I'm going to call in a prescription for prenatal vitamins. Please start them right away."

"Thank you," I say, letting my feet fall to the step when Vivian pushes in the extension.

"Unless there is anything else, I'll see you next month."

"Thanks again." Sofia shakes her hand.

14 EVER

I drive to the marina, placing the journal in my locker with the other pertinent records that I keep after I make sure I'm not being followed. My chef has prepared a steak on the grill and has dinner served on the upper deck. I've eaten out here every night since Noa and I made love in the lounger. It makes me feel closer to her, and right now, I want nothing more than to be holding her in my arms.

My mind skips to the pregnancy test, wondering if she used it this morning like she said?

Am I a father?

Am I capable of being one?

If my plan falls apart, I'll never lay eyes on the baby or Noa again. I will become as much of a danger to them as my father was to my mother, only not from me, but the hands of my family. It's the reason I never wanted children, but the thought of Noa having my baby brings me a joy inside I haven't experienced before. I can only imagine it's a small portion of what my mother felt. Her sole purpose became protecting me, and I'll do the same for my child even if I have to sacrifice being part of his or her life.

"This has to work." I exhale, collapsing on my bed, gripping my phone in my hand, wanting so badly to call Noa. "Hold on, baby," I say, dropping it on the bed, closing my eyes.

Nightmares haunt me, waking me up in a cold sweat at three in the morning. I toss and turn until five before I give up and head for a pot of coffee. I sip on a mug while scanning the details I have on Stanley Turro. His weakness is his sixteen-year-old daughter. I'd never harm her, but she'll be my pawn if things don't go as planned.

As soon as the clock hits nine, I dial Chief Bentley's office, and I'm put through immediately. "I have the journal in safekeeping. Once the deal goes down, I'll release it to you."

"Alright. I want you to know that you were correct in assuming one of your father's men would be by to check on our arrangement."

"Victor. He's going to be a problem."

"I gathered as much."

"Certainly you could have one of your men follow him and detain him for a few days."

"I'll assign a man to him, but I won't have him interfere if he's not doing something illegal. That's not how I operate."

"I understand, and believe it or not, I respect it."

"I've informed the FBI that you will be working with us, and they are fully on board with giving you your freedom, but in order to protect you from your family knowing you set them up, they'll arrest you along with your father and Nick."

"As long as I gain my freedom in the end, that's what matters."

"I'm going to text you the number to my direct line. Contact me when everything is in place."

"Will do."

Slipping my arm through my casual jacket, I finish dressing and opt for an open collar, no tie. The address Turro sent me leads to a strip club. I detest them. My father used to drag me to clubs and force me into the backrooms to watch. I hated how it made me feel so disconnected. Sex, as far as I was concerned, was emotionless. It was an act, nothing more. It's the reason I was able to dismiss women so easily all these years until Noa. She sparked a fire in me that I don't want extinguished. I crave her in every way possible. Today will be an uncomfortable reminder of my upbringing, but it will be the last time I ever step foot in a strip joint again.

I park outside the club and go over the numbers one more time before I exit my vehicle. It's your typical strip club dimly lit with patrons either in corners or right up front. It's not crowded this time of day, yet there are two ladies on stage. I recognize Turro from a photograph in his file.

Ordering a bourbon from the bar, I slide into the chair next to him, front and center.

"You must be Carmine's other son," he says, waving dollar bills.

"Yes."

"Your father was smart not to send Nick again. He's an arrogant asshole."

"I couldn't agree with you more." I chuckle.

One of the women on stage dances over to him, and he sticks the money in her string on her hip. She thanks him by baring her ass in his face and blowing him a kiss over her shoulder.

"I love women. All shapes and sizes," he growls, grabbing his crotch.

"If they are a distraction for you, we can discuss business elsewhere."

"I have a room in the back reserved." He stands, tucking in the tail of his shirt, and I follow him through the dark room, up a flight of stairs, and into a room with walls covered in red velvet. "This is where I choose to do business when I'm in town," he says, removing his jacket and getting comfortable on a black leather couch that I'm sure has seen its share of use.

I drag a wooden chair out of the hallway and sit directly in front of him. "Let's cut to the chase. The Leone organization has something you want. Why are you reluctant to pull the trigger, so to speak?"

"Because my ass is on the line if things go bad, and Nick was trying to renegotiate the deal. Your father and I agreed to a number, and he wanted more."

Interesting. Nick is taking money off of the top. "We can go back to the original number."

"Not good enough. There's a penalty for wasting my time. I could be balls-deep in the redhead on stage rather than in here with you."

"So what is it you want?"

"Twenty-five percent more."

"That's a lot."

"Take it or leave it. If you come back around again, it will go up another ten percent."

I think about the picture of his sixteen-year-old daughter, but I can't use her as a pawn. Chief Bentley and the FBI are going to stop the deal, so there's no real need to threaten him. "Twenty-five percent more. When can we deliver the goods?"

He narrows his eyes. "Just like that. You don't have to check with your old man?"

"He sent me to negotiate, and that's what I've done."

"You don't look or act like a Leone. Your father, Nick, and the other asshole that runs with him would be in here having an orgy. You sit there with well-manicured hands and didn't even look at the women on stage. How do I know this isn't some sort of set up?"

"My tastes are very different from theirs."

"So you like men?"

"No."

He picks up the phone next to him and calls for two women. "Prove it."

"I have nothing to prove to you." I stand. "If you don't want the deal, I'll have someone else lined up by the end of the day, and our profit will be higher. I was only trying to honor the deal my father had already made with you."

Two topless women slither into the room. One goes directly to his lap, and the other tries to peel me out of my jacket, but I push her away. "What's it going to be? I can guarantee you if you renege, my father has a code; there will be no future deals with your organization, and there will be a penalty to ensure your silence."

"I'll take the deal," he hisses.

"Since you've wasted my time, it will be at the original cost." I roll my sleeves up. "I'll meet you tomorrow on the docks at ten p.m. sharp. There will be a cargo ship in slot twenty-seven, loaded and ready for your direction."

"I'll want to check out the merchandise before it goes anywhere."

"I'd expect nothing less."

"Tell your father all future dealings will be with you. Not your greedy brother."

I wave dismissively over my shoulder and don't look back. "There won't be a next time," I mumble to myself, hurrying to get the hell out and ripping my coat off as soon as I get to the street. I sit in my car, taking deep breaths, trying to calm my racing heart.

"I can't believe I pulled it off." The next part should fall into place.

Driving off, I call Chief Bentley. "Tomorrow at the docks, ten o'clock, slot twenty-seven. Turro will be there to approve the merchandise."

"I'll have my men ready and waiting for them. Make sure you have the journal where I can find it."

"It will be in the trunk of my vehicle." I hang up.

I want to call Noa and tell her my nightmare is almost over, but I can't risk speaking to her for fear of what my family would do if they knew there was still a connection between the two of us. I fantasize for a moment what our lives could be like. I see us living in Essex in a cottage bigger than the one she owns with Sofia. At least a three-bedroom with a deck on the back larger than the house, overlooking the blue waters of the Atlantic. Two kids and a dog. I was never allowed a pet growing up. Nothing but love and happiness will fill our home. I'll have a legit job, a gorgeous loving wife, and not a care in the world.

I'm so lost in my thoughts while driving that I didn't see Nick following me until it was too late. He gets out of his car and walks the short distance in the marina parking lot, and taps a knuckle on my window.

There's a gun in my center console, but I opt to not grab it. I get out, and he's puffing on a cigarette.

"What are you doing here?"

"I could ask you the same thing."

"I wanted to see how it went with Turro. When I followed you from the strip club, I thought you'd be going to your apartment." He takes a hit of his cigarette and blows a white puff of smoke in the night air. "Victor told me he didn't believe you lived there, and where is your buddy Luca?"

"He and I parted ways. Not that it's any of Victor's fucking business, but I frequent the dive next to the marina. They have great food and hot women." I tilt my head in the direction I want his gaze to follow.

"It's a bit out of your way, don't you think?"

"What are you getting at, Nick?" I stand within inches of him. "I thought you and I buried the hatchet."

"I'd like to think so, but Victor keeps getting in my head. Why did you all of a sudden make an about-face when it comes to our business?"

"I don't know, Nick. What made you decide it was okay to skim money from our father?"

He takes a step back.

"Turro told me the deal you were trying to make

with him. So whatever beef you have with me, I suggest you get over it."

"Is that a threat?" He clenches his teeth, and his lip snarls.

"All I can say is that you'd better hope the deal goes through tomorrow, or I'll have to tell the old man the truth." I slam my car door and hit the button to lock it, and stroll in the direction of the restaurant.

I hear Nick say a few choice words then the sound of his tires spinning on the pavement is the next sound behind me. Walking through the doors, I meander to the bar and order a drink, and gulp it in one swig, wanting the burn. "Is there a back door?" I ask the bartender.

"Just past the restrooms," he answers.

I stride out the back and slowly move around the front of the single-story building, probing the parking lot of the marina to ensure Nick truly left. Once I'm sure the coast is clear, I bolt to the yacht and send a text to Luca.

KEEP *a close eye out on Noa. This should all be over by tomorrow night.*

15 NOA

I found my person, and he's changed me. The depth of love I feel for him is immeasurable. I don't want to admit that I can't breathe without him; that would make me weak. I've always been the strong independent type, but when I was with him, that woman no longer existed. How could I have craved him so much when he was right next to me.

I walked away from all these feelings when I left him, and now they are bottled up inside me, locked up, still wondering what comes after Ever? I've found my answer...new life.

"WHAT ARE YOU DOING IN HERE?" Sofia interrupts me, and I shut my laptop.

"I was trying to take your advice and distract myself by working on my blog."

"Oh, sorry. I could use some help at the restaurant today. Ricco has virtual meetings he's been called to attend."

"Have you forgiven him?"

"Cautiously, yes," she purses her lips.

"When this is all over, what's your future look like with him?"

"I honestly don't know. He'll ride off in the sunset, and I'll be here." She shrugs.

"That doesn't sound like a happy ending to me."

"The only happy ending I'm concerned with right now is yours, Ever's, and this baby." She pats my stomach.

"I pray that's in the cards for us. I can't stop worrying about Ever."

"I know. I'm concerned for you. Has Luca still not heard from him?"

"No."

"Can Ricco use his contacts to find out what's going on in New York?"

"I can call and ask him." She runs and gets her phone, and joins me in the middle of my bed.

When he picks up, she tells him he's on speakerphone. "Noa and I were wondering if you could use your contacts and garner any intel on what's going down in New York."

"I just got off the phone with my boss. He said that the FBI was contacted by the interim chief of police for backup concerning the Leone family. Apparently, Ever has negotiated a deal with him to hand him his father and his entire organization on a silver platter in exchange for his freedom."

I cover my mouth with my hand. "That means he's still alive."

"The deal is scheduled to go down tonight. If all goes as planned, he could have his life back shortly. He'll be arrested along with this family so they don't suspect his involvement. It will all be for show."

"He'll finally be free." A single tear runs down my cheek.

"That is the plan, barring any conflicts."

"Are you going to New York?" Sofia asks him.

"I begged for the assignment, but they want me here monitoring the two of you and Luca. I'll be notified as soon as it is finished."

"I'll book a flight to Manhattan so that I can be there when he's released."

"I'd strongly advise against it. Leone has your name on a hit list if you step foot in New York. Just because he'll be handcuffed doesn't mean it's safe for you to return."

"He's right. When it's safe, Ever will come to you." Sofia squeezes my knee.

I reluctantly agree to stay put.

"I'll let you know as soon as I hear the outcome," Ricco says, with a sweetness to his voice.

"Thank you. Perhaps when all is said and done, you and Ever could truly be brothers."

"It will be a shock to him that I exist."

"He's a good man, and at this point, I don't think anything would surprise him."

"I gotta go. I have another meeting starting."

"Thanks, Ricco," Sofia tells him, hanging up. "I hope that helped and didn't make things worse for you."

"The fact that he's alive gives me some measure of comfort."

"Good." She hops up. "Now, get your pregnant ass up and come help me at work."

"I'm going to go to the marina first, then I'll meet you at the restaurant. I want to update Luca. He deserves to be kept in the loop."

"I agree. See you afterward, but don't take too long. The lunch crowds haven't died down yet."

"I won't."

I skip out behind her and drive straight to the marina, and dart to the boat. "Luca!" I holler, and he comes barreling up the stairs, wiping shaving cream from his chin.

"What's wrong?"

"I have news about Ever." I take his hand, and we sit at the breakfast bar as I fill him in on what Ricco shared with me.

"I'm crossing my fingers for our boy," he says, hugging me. "You do realize a lot of things have to fall into place, and I hope like hell no one in his organization gets wind of it. It's far from over until the raid."

"I know, but I'm trying to think positive for my baby's sake."

"Are you still upset with me for not sending him the test results?"

"Yes, and no. I get why you felt you couldn't, and I'm sure you're right. It would have distracted him. So, you're forgiven.

"Thank you. I can't wait to see his face when you tell him in person."

"Do you think he's going to be happy?"

"It will give him a new lease on life. He adores you, and he's going to love this baby."

"Why don't you come by The Fork and Dough

later. I'll have our chef make whatever type of pizza you'd like on the house."

"Only if you'll join me at a table."

"Make it near closing time and we'll make it a celebration to the end of the Leone family name." I kiss his cheek and run down the dock to my car.

The restaurant is already busy, just like Sofia said it would be. Dawning a white apron, I help box up pizzas as the chef pulls them out of the oven. The phone is ringing off the hook, and we've all been too busy to answer it.

"I'll manage the phone for a bit," I tell Sofia and pick up the receiver. "The Fork and Dough, would you like to place an order?"

"Only if you'll be delivering it to me."

I gasp, covering the receiver. "Ever," I whisper.

"I know I shouldn't be calling you, but I needed to hear your voice. I'm calling from a pay phone outside of Manhattan. It took me two hours to find one still in use."

"I have so much I need to tell you about…"

"It will have to wait. I love you, baby."

"I love you too."

"Please hold on a little longer. It will all be over soon."

"I'm not going anywhere."

"Did you take the pregnancy test?"

I think about what Luca said about the results being a distraction to Ever. He's playing a deadly game and needs to maintain his focus. "I'm waiting for you to come home to me." It's only a partial lie. His deep sigh fills the moment of silence. "You can back out of whatever you've set in motion. There's another way out. Ricco—"

"I can't. It's too late. This is the only way out for me."

"But—"

"I'll come home to you when it's over. I'm sorry, baby, I can't stay on the line. I love you." He hangs up before I can respond.

"Damn it," I snap between clenched teeth.

"What's wrong?" Sofia sweeps her gaze in my direction without stopping what she's doing.

"Um…nothing." I decide not to tell her.

16 EVER

Tucking my .45 in my side holster, I adjust between the bulletproof jacket that Bentley provided me with and my shirt to ensure it can't be seen, along with a small pistol I add to my ankle holster. Grabbing an empty briefcase, I stop at the marina locker to pack the journal and other evidence into it, then place it where I told Bentley he could find it. Settling behind the wheel, I call my father on the way to the docks.

"Are you going to be waiting at home to celebrate the deal being done? I'll come by later, and we can celebrate together."

"Not on your life. This is a monumental deal for our organization. It will set us up for future business, and I'm going to make sure it goes smoothly."

That's exactly what I was hoping he'd say. "I suggest you keep Nick out of the picture." I know he won't.

"He'll be at my side, but I've instructed him to keep his mouth shut around Turro. I don't know what his beef is with him, but I intend to find out."

"Do you think he's capable of shutting his trap.?"

"He will, or I'll shoot him myself."

"What about Victor?"

"He's not part of the deal."

"Good. He's a cannon ready to be fired at any moment. I don't trust him as far as I can see him. I believe, given the chance, he'd turn on this family." I'm planting a seed of suspicion for him to take the fall.

"I'll have Nick deal with him. He brought him on board. He can kill him."

Never let it be said that Carmine Leone isn't a ruthless bastard. Seeing him cuffed and put in the back of an FBI unit will be the highlight of my life. He may not ever be found guilty of killing my mother, but at least he'll be paying the price for all the other crimes he's committed. "Congratulations on this deal."

"It wouldn't have gone through if it wasn't for you. I'm proud of you, Son."

Any other man would long to hear those words spoken from his father. It makes me sick to my stomach. "Just doing my job." I clear my throat of the words I really wanted to scream. "I'll meet you at the docks."

As I drive, all my thoughts are on Noa. I couldn't stop myself from calling her, thinking it could be the last time I ever got to hear her voice. She's the only reason I'm able to do any of this. If not for her, my hell would have no end.

I arrive at the docks first and check in on the cargo. The sun has fully set, and the only light comes from streetlights spaced eight feet apart and the dim lighting emanating from the cargo ship.

My father's vehicle arrives with his security team in tow at the same time as Turro's entourage. He and my father meet in the middle, shaking hands, and Nick stands beside him with a straight spine and one hand tucked behind his back.

"Thanks to your levelheaded son"—Turro cuts his sharp gaze to me—"this venture is going down. You might want to keep that other son of yours in line."

"I'm just glad we were able to seal the deal," I say firmly before he tells my father about Nick's attempt to steal from him.

"Without wasting any more time, I'd like to see what I purchased," Turro tells my father, and they walk up the steps of the ship.

"You didn't tell him," Nick says in a low voice.

"That you're stealing from him? No. He'll find out sooner or later without me ratting you out, brother." I glance at my watch. Bentley and the FBI should already be in place.

"I'll cut you in on the next deal if you make sure he doesn't," he says without moving his lips.

There won't be another deal. "We'll discuss percentages after this deal is done."

"I knew Victor was wrong about you, and I told him as much last night. He knows his time is limited with our organization."

Great, he lit the fuse to the cannon. "I'm glad you didn't bring him with you tonight. He's sure to stir up trouble."

"I didn't fill him in on it. When I last saw him a few hours ago, he was preoccupied by his dick being swallowed by some hooker."

"You need to fire him."

"You know there's no such thing in our organization. I'll arrange to have him…deleted." His lip curls. "You know, he truly almost had me convinced that you were playing a role to get back in the graces of our father only to expose us."

"He's a jealous ass," I grunt. "He'd get rid of both of us to get next to the great Carmine Leone."

"What convinced me is that you gave up the girl. I've tracked your phone and had you followed. If she'd have surfaced, I would've believed him. That and the fact that you killed a man. The old you wouldn't have taken someone else's life."

"It just took me a long time to fall into the Leone name." *I loathe him.*

"And a hell of a lot of beatings." He clasps my shoulder. "I didn't envy you, but I'm happy you finally saw the light. You and I could build a massive empire when the old man is gone. New York is just the tip of the iceberg."

"Great minds think alike. We need to expand." The only place he'll be going is prison.

"I'm going to go make sure everything is going as planned."

I grab his arm, halting him. "Stay out of it. Turro doesn't like you, and you'll risk him backing out."

"You have a good point." He strikes a match, lighting a cigarette.

Out of the corner of my eye, I see a shadow of a man near my car at my trunk. *What the hell?* As I raise my foot to move, bright lights shine in our faces, and we're swarmed by agents.

"Drop to the ground!" a man's voice barks, surrounding us with an army of men.

I raise my hands and go to one knee.

Nick reaches for his weapon and runs for cover, then all hell breaks loose. Gunfire comes from Turro's men. Nick screams out in pain when he takes a bullet to his right shoulder. I'm caught in the crossfire, lying flat on the ground. Bodies from both sides are falling around me.

Bentley's men, locked and loaded, take the walkway up to the ship where my father and Turro went to check the cargo. I hear shouting and gunfire and see pops of orange in the air. An explosion has my ears ringing and flames darting out of the ship. Debris flies through the air with a hot piece of metal scalding my leg.

Slinging it from my leg, the orange metal rolls on the wood dock, landing against a body. Stumbling to get to my feet, I see Turro's body floating in the water facedown. Shielding myself behind a container, I snatch my gun that's loaded with blanks, firing like I'm protecting Nick.

"Over there!" Nick yells, showing me an agent with a direct line of fire on our men who are running to get away from the flames that are now twenty feet in the air, lighting up the docks.

In one quick move, I shoot and run, landing in a roll, then twist to my feet next to Nick. "We're outnumbered, and if any more of the explosives go off, we're all going up in flames.

"I'd rather die than be hauled off to prison for the rest of my life." Nick takes a long hard look at me. "Did you set this up?" he spits. "It had to be you. Victor was right all along."

"You're being paranoid. Why would I put myself in the middle of this shit to be taken down too?"

He aims his weapon at me, and I raise my hands. "No one else knew about this meeting. It had to be you!"

"You're wrong." I see movement by my car again. "Victor," I snarl. "He did this. You said he didn't know about the meeting, then why the hell is he here!"

Nick pokes his head out enough to see him. "The bastard set us up! I'm going to kill him!" He grips his shoulder, getting to his feet, and a bullet nearly hits him in the head.

"Stay down," I bark, shoving him to the ground. "I'll take care of him. Victor pops open my trunk and snatches the briefcase. "Shit!" Taking out the loaded pistol from my ankle holster, I move, staying low to the ground out of the gunfire, making my way toward Victor. When I round the corner, I don't see him, and it's grown silent other than the raging sound of the fire. My father is on his knees with his arms twisted behind his back, being cuffed along with several of Turro's men. Nick isn't where I left him.

"I have to find Victor," I mumble, creeping along the containers, searching for him. One of Bentley's men jumps out in front of me.

"You're under arrest," he says.

A shot rings out, and he hits the ground with an eerie thud. Then a heavy metal door springs open, slamming into my face, knocking me to the ground, and sending my gun flying into the water. Victor jumps on top of me. "You crossed the wrong man!" He speaks so hard that his spit splatters in my eyes. He rears back, and the butt of his gun connects with my forehead, and then he covers my face with a rag. I struggle to get free, but my head starts to spin, and my vision fades. "You're going to pay for this," is the last thing I remember hearing.

MY TEMPLES THROB, and wetness drips down my face. "Where the hell am I?" I rasp in a scratchy, dry voice, then vomit.

It's pitch black, and I can't make out anything. Steadying my hands beneath me, I get to my knees. I try to stand but bang my head on something, knocking me back to the concrete floor. Holding my hands out, I search for a wall or something to hold on to, only to find thick metal bars, and fear bristles over my skin as my limbs begin to shake as rapid breathing takes over. The sound of my own heartbeat thrashes in my ears, and pure panic fills me.

I know this place all too well. I'm in the cage my father built for me, where my hell began.

17 NOA

"Why haven't we heard anything by now?" I've paced a path on the checkered tile floor.

"It's too soon. Come sit and try to eat something," Ricco says.

"I can't eat. I'm too worried."

"You should try." Luca pats the spot next to him in the booth. "The pizza is amazing."

I fall in the seat and lay my head on the table, and he rubs my shoulders. "The waiting is killing me," I whine.

"You need to eat for the baby's sake." Sofia reaches across the table, taking my hand in hers.

I lift my head and sit tall. "Ever is out there living through god knows what. I can't eat."

Ricco juggles for the pager on his hip when it goes off. "I need to make a phone call," he says when he reads the message, having Sofia stand so that he can get out of the booth.

"I pray that's word on Ever. It's nearly midnight. It should all be long over by now."

"It will be," Luca's eyes are filled with as much concern as mine.

"I spoke with him today." I whisper my admission.

"What?" Luca turns in his seat to look at me.

"He called the number here from a pay phone, so it couldn't be traced."

"What did he say?" he asks while Sofia remains silent, waiting for me to answer.

"He said he needed to hear my voice, that he loved me, and told me to hold on a little longer." I sigh, letting a single tear slip down my cheek.

"I'm so glad you got to speak with him." Sofia smiles.

"Me too," I sniff.

Sofia picks up a piece of pizza and holds it out in front of me. "Just a bite or two."

I know she's right; I need to eat for the baby. I bite off the end of it and catch the cheese with my hand. "It is good," I mumble with my mouth full.

Ricco strides with purpose back into the dining area with a deep worry line creasing his forehead. "I've been ordered to go to New York."

"What happened?" Sofia is on her feet.

He squats to the side of me. "The deal went down, and they have Carmine in custody."

Sofia's hand covers her heart. "Thank God."

"What aren't you telling us?" I frown.

"There was a lot of gunfire, and it set off a round of explosions, lighting the shipyard on fire."

"Ever?"

"They haven't found him…or his body."

I scramble to my feet, nearly knocking him over. "He could've escaped."

"Are they still searching for Ever?" Luca questions him.

"They'll have a better idea of what they are dealing with in the light of day. They're concentrating on containing the fire and pulling bodies out of the water."

A swell of tears fills my eyes, threatening to burst. "You said they have Carmine. What about Nick and Victor?"

Ricco shakes his head. "The chief of police said that Nick was shot, but he wasn't sure how badly he was hurt. He wasn't amongst the bodies that have been recovered either."

"When are you leaving?" Sofia stands in front of him.

"Tonight."

"I'm going with you," I blurt out.

"Like hell you are." Ricco scowls.

"You can't stop me. If Carmine is in custody, then I have no reason to not get on a plane."

"If you're going, so am I. I'm not letting you out of my sight until Ever is found." Luca slides out of the booth.

"You guys aren't leaving without me," Sofia crosses her arms over her chest and juts her chin.

I move in front of her, placing my hands on the outside of her arms. "You have to stay here. We can't shut down the restaurant, or we'll lose all the business you've worked so hard to get. Besides, with Ever's father behind bars, I'll be alright."

"I'll see to it," Luca assures her.

"Fine!" She drops her arms to her side and then raises a finger to point at me. "The minute any of you know anything, you're to call me."

"I will." Ricco steps between us. "As soon as I know, you will too."

"Leave your car here. I'll drive you to your house to pack a bag," Luca says.

"You can't fly on the FBI jet. You'll have to arrange your own flight. When you have it, text me the details, and I'll have a car waiting to pick you up."

"Mr. Christianson has a private plane on standby for me whenever I need it," Luca tells Ricco. "I'll make a phone call on the way to Noa's place."

"Alright. I'll see the two of you in New York." He tugs Sofia to the side and whispers something to her, followed by a kiss.

"Let's go." I wave for Luca to follow me out the door. We rush to his car, and he speeds down the road as he connects with his phone, calling the pilot. I'm antsy as hell with all sorts of thoughts ramming through my mind. What if we're too late? Is he hurt, hiding somewhere, bleeding out with no one by his side?

"Stop whatever scenario you have playing in your head," Luca says, glancing at me. "We're going to find him."

"You can call him," I say, picking up his phone.

"If he's hiding or someone has taken him, it might give his location away. We should wait for now."

"But, what if he needs us?"

He gnaws on the inside of his cheek. "Fine. Call him."

I scroll to his name and push the green phone button. It rings several times and goes to voicemail. "Ever. Where are you? I'm worried sick. Please call me. I'm headed your way." I hang up, and my insides are trembling. "He has to be okay. I don't want to raise this baby without him."

He parks at my place, and I race inside and grab essentials only. I'm tossing my bag in his trunk within minutes.

"All I have to do is run into the boat and snatch my bug-out bag. Ever has insisted I keep one at all times since I started driving for him."

"He knew this day would come at some point."

"I believe he did," he says, turning into the marina parking lot. "Come inside with me. I'm not leaving you out here alone."

I unbuckle and follow him inside. He disappears and reappears shortly, handing me a small gun. "I want you to keep this on you at all times. It will fit in your purse. Do you know how to use it?"

"My father taught me the basics," I take it from him, check the safety, and hold it until we get back in the car and stuff it into my purse.

"The pilot will have the plane ready for takeoff in an hour."

"Do you really believe that Ever is okay?" My lip quivers.

"Ever has survived far worse things in his life. If anyone made it out, he did."

"I pray you're right." I cup my belly with the palm of my hand. "He has people who are counting on him."

When we arrive at the private airport, Luca takes both of our bags and tosses them in the plane, and ushers me inside as he goes to find the pilot.

The plane holds four single seats and a row of seating that appears to hold two more passengers. It's all crisp white and very clean. There is a stack of vintage books on a low shelf by the seats with a lip holding them in place. Each space is equipped with a tablet and headphones.

I take a seat by the window and roll up the shade to only see the runway lights. A few minutes later, Luca is strapping into the seat that faces me. "We'll be taking off shortly. Once we are in the air, the flight will be approximately two hours long. I suggest you try to get some rest."

"Are these Ever's?" I ask, touching the spine of one of the books.

"Yes. He loves the classics. The Great Gatsby is his favorite."

"Jay Gatsby's obsession with Daisy Buchanan," I recite the names from memory.

"It reminds me of yours and Ever's story. Set in New York, millionaire in love, and his fight for you."

"I guess it sort of does," I say, picking up the book, clinging it to my chest, and resting my head against the seat back.

The plane takes off, and I'm lulled to sleep from pure exhaustion, still holding on to the book.

"NOA. WE'VE LANDED," Luca says, shaking my shoulder gently.

I blink a few times, wipe the drool from the corner of my mouth and pick the book up from my lap, putting it back on the shelf. "That was quick."

He laughs. "You slept the entire time. Ricco's driver is waiting."

"Where is he taking us?"

"I don't know, but we are about to find out."

He picks up our bags, and I cling to my purse as we exit. A completely blacked-out SUV is parked off the skirts of the runway. Luca tosses our bags in the trunk, and he holds the door open for me to climb in the back seat. I scoot all the way over, and he gets in with me.

"Luca," he tells the driver, extending his hand over the front seat. "This is Ms. Sutton."

He acknowledges both of us. "I've been instructed to take you to Agent Ricco."

"And where might that be?" Luca asks, buckling up.

"He's shored up in a hotel near the shipyard."

"Thank you," he tells him and then holds my hand for the duration of the ride in silence.

As soon as we're parked, the doors fly open, and we are ushered securely with our belongings to the sixth floor. Ricco and several other men dressed in black with FBI vests on are in the room, gathered around a table filled with papers.

"You made it safely," Ricco greets Luca with a handshake and a raised lip smile for me.

"You look worn out," I tell him.

"They'll be no rest until this ordeal is over."

"Any update on Ever?" Luca and I follow him to the table.

"I'm afraid nothing good." He points to the large blueprint of the shipyard. "According to one of our men whose job it was to know the whereabouts of

Mr. Christianson during the takedown, he was last seen here." He aims a finger at a map. "Our agent lost him after the second explosion when he was seriously injured. Ever was hunkered down with Nick, who had taken a bullet in the shoulder."

"Where exactly was the explosion?" Luca leans down for a better look at the blueprint.

"Here." One of the other agents indicates with the tap of his finger.

"So, if Mr. Christianson was here and the explosion was here." He draws a line with his finger. "It's very possible he was unaffected."

"Yes, but the first explosion could have gravely injured him. He was lying flat on the ground not far from it."

"He was able to move to here," I say, tapping the blueprint where they showed him previously.

"True," he responds. There was a trail of blood left behind that led to the water."

"It could have been Nick's. Have they found his body?"

"No. So far, we've identified several of Carmine's security team, Turro's men, and Stanley Turro himself. We've raided Leone's place of business, and any remaining associates have either been arrested or have disappeared.

The door opens, and a man wearing a badge strolls into the room. "Unfortunately, he can't make any further arrests until we find the journal Mr. Christianson was providing us. His father already had his attorney at his side and is trying to post bail."

"Surely they won't grant it," I gasp.

"And who are you?" He angles toward me.

Luca steps beside me. "I'm Mr. Christianson's employee, and this is Noa Sutton, an associate of his."

"A judge won't hear his case until morning," he finally states. "Mr. Christianson made my department aware that the judges in Manhattan were owned by the Leone organization, so I had to petition to bring someone in from another area, and it has stalled his progress."

"You said Ever was providing you his father's journal," I interject.

"That was the agreement. He told me it would be in the trunk of his car, but when the takedown was over, I found his car with the trunk open and empty. I believe he took the evidence and left town."

"He wouldn't do that! He wanted to see his father behind bars," Luca snaps.

"Someone else must have known where he put it." I tap my finger to my lip. "Was Victor found among the bodies? I don't recall you saying his name."

"No, he was not, and Ever warned me about him, that he could be trouble. As far as we know, he wasn't at the scene at any time."

"Excuse me, sir," an agent interrupts him. "When I interviewed the agent that was watching Mr. Christianson, he said he saw an unidentified man by his vehicle right before the explosion."

"I'm betting that someone was Victor." Ricco gets on the phone.

"That's who you need to be searching for. Find him, and I bet you'll find Ever," I say.

18 EVER

A bright light floods the room, blinding me. Shielding my eyes and turning my head away, I hear voices.

"I told you it was him who set it up. Why else would he be wearing a bulletproof vest?" It's Victor's gravelly voice.

I touch my chest, and my shirt is gone.

"You were right all along." It sounds like Nick punches a wall. "Ah!" he snaps. "My fucking shoulder!"

"You're going to have to let me doctor it. You can't go to a hospital. Your name is all over the news."

"What do you know about gunshot wounds?"

"Not a damn thing," Victor states.

"He does."

I haven't been able to focus yet, but I imagine he's pointing at me.

"I've seen him treat some of our men before."

"I'm not letting him out," Victor spats.

"What the hell are we going to do with him?" The sound of his footsteps moves him closer to me.

"I say we torture him like your father used to. Isn't that what he built this thing for?" He rattles the cage with both hands.

"Water, please," I rasp, coughing.

"You don't deserve shit after what you've done!" Nick yells.

"It wasn't me."

"Sure it wasn't." Victor laughs.

Nicks squats, looking through the bars. "How do you explain the vest?"

"I told you Victor was a loose cannon. I knew he'd show up, and I'd be his target. I wore it for protection from him."

Nick glances over his shoulder at Victor.

"Then how do you explain having your father's journal in the trunk of your vehicle? I followed you and saw where you stashed it."

"I suspected he contacted the authorities, and I knew our building would be raided and that they'd be tailing our father based on the information he gave them. I waited until our father left work, and I followed him to the subway station to the locker you told me about. I was trying to save our asses from the likes of him." My gaze, still a little fuzzy, fixates on Victor.

"He's lying to you!" Victor kicks the cage. "His meeting with the chief of police was a charade. He had no intention of getting him on our team. He used the situation to set this whole thing up!"

"Think about it, Nick. Why would I have given up everything to turn around and ruin it? Our livelihood is gone, and we're now fugitives. The empire we were building is in total ruins. I'm sure all our assets have been seized and our accounts frozen."

"I bet the girl isn't out of the picture at all. I'll find her and prove it to you." Victor's eyes are filled with rage.

Nick walks in a circle and then reverses his direction. "I don't know who to believe."

"Let me torture him, and I'll get the truth out of him," Victor growls.

"I am telling you the truth. He set me up because he knew he had exceeded his time with our family. It's his way of paying us back." I keep my voice on an even keel to be convincing. "He should be the one in this cage, not me. Better yet, he should be floating in the river with Turro. If any of his men survived, they'll be coming after all of us."

"He's got a point." Nick pulls a gun from his belt, leveling it at Victor.

"Hey, man," he says, showing Nick the palms of his hands.

"Kill him," I say.

"You shut the fuck up!" Victor screams. "He's messing with your head, man. Give me a chance to prove he's lying. I'll get the girl and bring her to you. She'll squeal like a stuck pig if we threaten her family."

"The woman's been out of my life since she packed her ass on a plane. I haven't seen or spoken to her since. She's got nothing to do with any of it."

"Then it won't harm anything to have a face-to-face chat with her," Nick says, lowering the gun.

"As soon as I find her, I'll bring her to you and force her to talk."

"Go," Nick orders, waving him off with the gun.

Shit. I've got no way to warn her. "Since you're on the fence about me, may I please have some water? You might as well keep me alive until you find out the truth."

He stomps up the basement stairs and returns

with a bottle of room temp water. "Here." He hands it to me through the bars.

"Thanks." I twist off the cap and take a few swallows. "I can treat your shoulder if you want."

"It hurts like a son of a bitch." He cradles it close to his chest.

"Your choice. You can either let me help you or risk getting an infection and possibly lose your arm." I shrug and gulp down more water.

"I don't trust you."

"Alright," I say, sitting. "When you're in agony, you'll change your mind."

"How did you survive this?" He reaches up with his uninjured arm and pulls down a bar my father used to hang me from by my wrists high enough that my feet wouldn't touch the floor. "You were just a kid."

"At the time, I hated him. I had enough strength in me that I wasn't going to let him win."

"At what point did you finally concede? Was it the beatings with the whip or the hours being shackled to this contraption?"

"Believe it or not, I got to where I didn't feel the pain anymore."

"Then what was it that broke you?"

"When he filled that tub with water"—I point to

the rusted container—"and drowned me only to have me resuscitated to repeat the process."

"Damn," he mutters like it's news to him. "That would have broken me too."

"Did you know he killed my mother?"

He runs his hand along the bars as he walks around the cage. "Not until many years later. I overheard him talking about it. That's when I knew I didn't want to cross him."

"So, what changed your mind?" I chuckle. "I mean, you were trying to skim money from him with the Turro deal."

"Victor." He blows out a long breath. "He convinced me that I was worth more than the old man was forking out."

"And yet, somehow, I'm the one locked in this cage. He's been setting you up all along."

"I can't think. I need to get the hell out of here," he shuffles off up the stairs leaving the light on.

I examine each spindle of the cage, recalling breaking out of it once when I found one of them loose. I didn't get far before I was caught and beaten again.

"It was this one," I mutter to myself, pulling as hard as I can on the bar. "He fucking welded it!" I bang my head on the side. "I've got to find a way out of here to warn Noa." Searching the room for anything within reaching distance I can use, I see a hammer. Squeezing my arm through all the way up to my shoulder and extending my fingers, I still can't reach it. "Damn it!" I wail.

Nick falters down the stairs, looking a little gray. "I don't feel so good." He's dragging the first aid kit that has been kept in this house since I was a child.

"Let me help you," I say, pleading with him.

He digs in his pocket and pulls out a key unlocking the cage, then grabs his gun. "Don't try anything."

"I only want to help you." I hold my hands in the air. I get to my feet and bend low so as not to hit my head again.

"I swear if you make one wrong move…"

"I won't," I say, standing tall once I've cleared the cage. "Give me the first aid kit."

He hands it to me, then sits in the wooden chair that I've been tortured in numerous times. Slowly, I take out the supplies I need. "Your shirt has to come off."

He lays the gun in his lap and takes it off, then picks up the gun again. Picking up a vial, I read the label. "Lidocaine, but it's well past its expiration date."

"I don't need anything for pain. Just get the damn bullet out."

Unsheathing the scalpel, I pour alcohol into his wound, and he hisses, baring his teeth. "Fuck!" he yells.

He keeps the gun pointed at me as I slice open the bullet hole. "It's lodged in the bone. This is going to hurt like a mother." I can only hope he passes out and drops the gun.

Digging the scalpel in harder than I need to, he screams in pain. "Sorry, it's really deep."

His eye flutter, and his grip on his gun loosens. I keep applying pressure until his head falls back and his eyes are closed. Dropping the scalpel, I search his pocket for a phone and car keys.

I go to run up the stairs and stop, looking around the basement. "I'll never be held captive in here again." An old kerosine lantern hangs from a corner. At times, it was the only light I had. Taking it down, I shake it, listening for the sound of liquid. Unscrewing it, I pour its contents around the room and find Nick's lighter. Heaving him over my shoulder, I carry him upstairs and toss him on the couch. Returning to the basement, I flick the lighter and toss it, igniting the fluid.

"Good riddance." I shut the door and hear the click of a gun.

"Where do you think you're going?" Nick's head bobbles.

I dart through the room, but not before he gets a shot off, nicking me in the side where the vest comes together. The sting takes the wind out of me, and I stumble, smearing blood against the wall.

"Admit it. It was you, wasn't it!" He's on his feet, standing in front of the door to the basement.

I stand tall. "Yes. I'm the one who informed the FBI of the meeting." His hand wavers, and he gets off another round before I make impact with him. Shoving him through the door, he falls down the stairs, cracking his head on the concrete, and flames dance around him. I hesitate, not wanting to see him die.

"I'm going to kill you!" he snarls, trying to get to his feet.

I lower my head and shut the door. Grappling with the keys, I jam them into the ignition and call Noa. "Pick up the phone," I growl. When it goes to voicemail, I try Luca's number, and it does the same thing. "Damn it!" I switch over, calling Bentley.

"My brother is in the basement of my father's house. Send a firetruck and an ambulance."

"We've already raided your father's place. There was no one there."

"The house on Baker Street, not the one in town."

"Where the hell are you?"

"I'm going after Victor." He starts to say something, but I hang up. Popping open the glove box, I find the pistol I was carrying and my phone. Turning it on while I drive, I listen to a voicemail from Noa.

"EVER. *Where are you? I'm worried sick. Please call me. I'm headed your way.*"

"NO! NO! NO!" I beat on the dash. "Don't come to New York!" I call her back, and it goes directly to her voicemail again.

"Wherever you are, go somewhere safe. Victor is after you, and if he finds you"—I choke—"just please get out of New York, and if you're in Essex, have Luca take you out in the boat and don't come to shore until you hear from me again."

19 NOA

I stand back, listening to the conversations going around among the men in the room. Chief Bentley puts out an APB on Victor. Ricco reviews the details of the explosion, and Luca is actively asking questions. One agent, the younger of the men, walks out of the room, pressing his ear to the phone.

"Excuse me. I need to use the ladies' room." I tug on an agent's arms.

"It's down the hall on the left."

"Thank you." I find it and shut the door, and wash my face. I hear a voice coming through a vent and can make out every other word, one which includes Ever's name. I climb on the sink and get closer to the vent to hear the dialog.

. . .

"THE PLAN IS to arrest him and then set him free after the organization is taken down." He's quiet for a moment. "You're directing me to make sure he doesn't make it into the back of a police car. You want him dead."

I GULP, my hand trembling over my mouth. Climbing down, I snug my purse under my arm and peek out the door. The younger agent I saw leaving the room emerges from the door next to the bathroom, and he's tucking his phone to the clip on his belt.

"I have to tell Luca," I whisper. Licking my lips, I walk back into the room, and Luca is in a deep discussion with Ricco. "I really need to speak with the two of you," I say, glancing over at the young agent who is standing over the table listening to an exchange of ideas.

"Alright," Ricco acknowledges what I said.

"Not here. Can we go out into the hallway?"

They step away with me, but Ricco's team pulls him back in with questions, so it's just me and Luca.

"I overheard one of the agents taking orders from

someone who wants Ever dead instead of bringing him to the authorities."

"A rogue agent."

"At this point, I don't trust any of them but Ricco."

"I believe Bentley is on Ever's side."

"Are you kidding me? He thinks Ever double-crossed him taking the journal."

"I'll keep my ears open. When we go back inside, I want you to go stand behind the man that you overheard talking."

"Then what?"

"I'll inform Ricco."

He opens the door, and I casually stand behind the agent. Luca drags Ricco to the side, and then he storms over toward the agent. "I need you to clear the room," he commands me.

Before I exit, Ricco has the agent against the wall, pinned with his forearm pressing on his neck. "Get his phone," he yells, and another agent snaps it off its clip. "Who gave you orders to kill Ever?"

The man's jaw visibly tightens, but he doesn't answer him.

"You sorry piece of shit!" Ricco spits in his face. "Trace the last number on his phone."

"I'm going to let you guys deal with it. Ever called

and reported where Nick could be found. My men are there now, and I want to question him," Bentley states, adjusting his holster.

"I'm going with you," I say, firmly enough he's not about to tell me any differently.

He looks at Ricco, who nods. "Suit yourself, but you are in no way to hinder anything."

I turn toward Luca. "Stay here and find him. I'll be alright with Bentley."

"Okay. Have him bring you back here as soon as he's done."

"I will." I follow Bentley to his squad car, and he has me get in the front seat. "Where is Nick?"

"In the house that he and Ever grew up in."

A cold, sweaty chill runs down my spine.

"According to what my men have been able to ascertain from Nick, he and Victor drugged Ever at the shipyard and took him to the house. My men had searched the current house the Leone family owns, but apparently, he still has the title to their old home, but under a different name.

"I wonder why he kept it?"

"Who knows with a criminal mind like Leone's."

The drive takes us to the outskirts of town to a large gray house surrounded by a wrought iron fence. He parks, and we're greeted by several officers. "Where is he?" Bentley asks.

"He's cuffed in the living room. The paramedics want to take him to the hospital."

"If he's not dying, he needs to be interrogated first," he grumbles, and I follow him into the house.

As soon as Nick sees me, he starts screaming. "I knew it! The bastard lied about everything! You're the reason he did this! I've lost everything because of you!"

"Calm his ass down," Bentley growls. He starts asking him questions, and I meander through the house. The chill returns when I'm standing in front of a door that has yellow tape mounted to it.

"You can't go in there, ma'am. It's not safe."

"There was a fire? Is this where they found him?"

The fireman nods and drags his gear behind him.

I duck under the tape, and the smell of smoke lingers in the room. The stairs look untouched by the fire. Cautiously, I pat down them. Black char mars the space, and there's a haze of smoke lingering near the ceiling. In the middle of the room is a metal cage, and I swallow the burn of bile in my throat. "This is where he tortured you." How could a father be so cruel?" My throat fills with bile at the thought of what they did to him.

There's a bar hanging from the ceiling with rusted chains and blood stains on the bare concrete floor. "He chained you up so you couldn't fight him. The torture he must have endured is unimaginable," I cry. Not being able to handle any more, I dart up the stairs and storm over to Nick and slap him hard across the face.

"How dare you bring him back to this hellish nightmare! Did you lock him in that cage?" My heart breaks for Ever.

He lifts his uninjured shoulder to his cheek and then laughs with a disgusting smile on his lips. "You should have seen how pathetic he looked, just like he did when he was a kid. It brought back all sorts of memories for me. Think how much it's fucked up his head."

I've never wanted to harm someone so badly in my life. I thrust forward to get my hands around his neck, but Bentley snags me by the arms before I can get to him again. "I hope you rot in hell!"

Bentley threatens to cuff me as he ushers me out of the house. "I know you're angry, but this isn't helping. I'll have one of my men drive you back into town. Nick isn't going anywhere but to prison with the confessions he's made."

I shrug free of him. "I'll hail a cab."

He bites his bottom lip and holds his hands in the air. "Alright."

I walk as fast as I can to the gated entrance and make it a few blocks before I can flag a cab down. "If Ever is injured, where would he go?"

I free my phone from my purse, wanting to call him again. "Dang it. It's dead." Then the answer to my question comes to me. I swing open the back door of the cab and give him directions. "That's going to be an expensive fair," he calculates the cost on his computer.

"It doesn't matter. Just get me there as fast as you can. Do you have a phone charger I can use?"

He opens his middle console and hands me a cord. "There's a spot to plug it in the back seat."

"Thanks."

He pulls out into traffic, and I wait for my phone to have enough charge to light it up. I hold my breath when I see I have a voicemail. My heart races, waiting to listen to it.

"WHEREVER YOU ARE, *go somewhere safe. Victor is after you, and if he finds you—*" I hear him choke on his words. *"Just please get out of New York, and if you're in Essex, have Luca take you out in the boat, and don't come to shore until you hear from me again."*

"EVER," I silently cry. I switch over to text and send Luca a message.

I'VE GONE SOMEWHERE *safe and hope to find Ever.*

LUCA IS GOING to be so pissed that I left, but he's where he needs to be helping Ricco. If Victor is after me, it would only put his life in more danger because I know he'd sacrifice his own life for me to keep Victor from harming me. He won't find me where I'm going.

THE TRAFFIC WAS HEAVY, and the normal two-hour drive from Manhattan to West Hampton Dunes took nearly three hours.

"Are you sure this is the right place? It doesn't look like anyone lives in the mansion," the cab driver peers out the window.

"This is it," I state, handing him cash.

Unbuckling, I throw my purse over my shoulder and run up the steps of the house and grab the doorknob, but it's locked. After the cab driver leaves, I peek through the window. "Ever!" I yell his name in despair.

I don't see any signs of movement. My sandals hit the steps hard, and I run through the grass to the white gate on the side yard, where the grass turns to white sand. Slipping off my shoes, I trek to the back of the house and onto the deck. "Ever!" I scream his name again.

The glass doors are locked too. There's a long narrow window on either side of the doors. Digging through the sand, I find a rock and break the glass, carefully slipping my hand inside and unlocking the sliding glass doors. Rushing inside, I check every room. The place is just as we left it. There are no sandy footprints on the floor other than mine.

"Why aren't you here!" I cry. My phone rings, and I snatch it to my ear. "Ever!"

"What the hell were you thinking? Where are you?" Luca says

"I had a voicemail from Ever telling me that Victor is searching for me and that I needed to get somewhere safe. I had an idea of where I might find Ever, but I was wrong."

"Tell me where you are so that I can come get you."

"No. I don't want you in any more danger. I'm safe. You keep trying to locate Ever."

"Noa, if anything happens to you, I'll never forgive myself."

"And I feel the same about you. You'd die before you'd let Victor take me, and I'm not going to allow that to happen."

"Just tell me where you are?" His voice is laced with desperation.

"For your own safety, I'm not going to tell you, and I certainly don't want to verbalize it on your phone because, at this point, it could be bugged. I'll text you if I find him, and you do the same. Goodbye, Luca." I hang up before he can argue with my logic.

Taking a glass from the kitchen cabinet, I turn on the faucet and fill it. Checking the pantry, there's no food. "I really need to feed you, little one." I peer at my stomach. I put my location in my phone and map quest my surroundings. "There's a tiny market a couple miles down the road. The last time I was here, I recall there being a couple of bikes left in the garage when Ever and I toured the place." I snap my fingers and take the hallway leading to the garage.

Flipping on the light in the garage, I see them. One has a flat tire, but the other one looks okay. Rolling it out the side door, I climb on and pedal the driveway winding onto the one-lane paved road, running down the island. I'm thankful for a somewhat overcast day, keeping the midday sun at bay.

Parking the bike against the tan building, I go inside and load a paper bag with food items and a couple bottles of orange juice. Once I'm balanced on the bike with my purse over my shoulder, and the bag gripped in one hand, I head back to the house. Instead of returning the bike to the garage, I ride it through the gate and rest it against the lower part of the deck.

As I step up onto the deck, I stop in my tracks. There's another set of footprints leading into the house, and the sliding glass doors are open. Easing the paper bag to the ground, I reach inside my purse and take out the handgun, shifting the safety switch off.

I tiptoe into the house with my gun gripped in both hands out in front of me. Easing my way into the living room, I look behind the sofa and chairs and swing open the coat closet. I jump when I hear a noise in the kitchen. Patting my way over the plush carpet, I turn into the kitchen, and there's someone standing with the fridge door open. All I can see is their legs.

"You've got two seconds to get out of this house before I start shooting," I stammer with my hands trembling.

A head pops up, and hands are held high. "It's me," he says and slowly closes the door.

"Ever!" I cry and rush into his arms, nearly knocking him over. "I knew you'd come here," I say, kissing his face with tears of relief streaming down my cheeks.

"You shouldn't fucking be here, but I'm so glad you are." He embraces either side of my face with his hands and crashes his lips to mine.

20 EVER

"Wait." She pulls back, her bottom lip already swollen from my brutal kiss. "Are you okay? Are you hurt? You look like crap." Her gaze skims over my body as she talks quickly. "Oh my god, you've been shot." She turns me to the side, and I wince when she touches my wound. "I'm so sorry."

"Slow down. The bullet only grazed me."

"You need stitches." She points to my brow.

"If you'll just let me hold you, I promise I'll be alright." I fold her into my arms, and she lays her head on my shoulder.

"I've been so worried about you." She trembles in my arms.

"Does anyone know you are here?"

She shakes her head. "I had to break in."

"I saw that." I kiss her forehead.

"I remembered there was a bike in the garage. I needed to get some food."

"When you came in wielding a gun at me, I was putting a few things in the fridge."

"You scared me. I thought somehow Victor found me."

"You did get my message."

Tears fill her eyes with something more than sadness. "I saw the basement." Her voice quivers, and I realize that "something more" is the pain she feels for me.

I ease her off my chest and hold her at arm's length, blinking a few times. "How?"

"Chief Bentley wanted to interrogate Nick."

"He's still alive then." I run my hand through my hair. "How did you even end up in Manhattan?"

She weaves her hand in mine and leads me to the couch. "Ricco is an undercover FBI agent."

"I suspected there was more to his story."

"So much more than you know," she mumbles.

Curling my thumb beneath her chin, I lift it so that she has to look me in the eye. "Tell me."

"Ricco's father is Carmine Leone. His mother was used by him as a young, lost teenage girl. She got pregnant and never told him. Like your mother's story, she moved him as far away from Carmine as she could. This was before your mother. He's five years older than you."

"Damn. I have a brother on the good guys' side."

She cups my face. "You're on that same team. He wanted to help you escape your family. He had a file on you that had horrific details of your life growing up in that house. Before he joined the FBI, you were their pawn to get to your father. They used you in the worst way. Seeing that basement gutted me, and I wanted to kill Nick myself."

"That part of my life is behind me now."

"You set the basement on fire, didn't you?"

"I wish the entire house would have burnt down."

"It's all over now, right?"

"Not until I find Victor and get my hands on my father's journal. That's the deal I made with Bentley for my freedom."

"We're safe here." She curls into my arms.

I see the paper bag of groceries next to the door. "Have you eaten today?"

"I'm only hungry for you," she purrs.

"You'll not have me until there is food in your stomach." I push her to a sitting position and stare at her stomach. "Why didn't you take the pregnancy test?"

"I lied when I told you I hadn't. I was afraid my answer would distract you." She gets to her feet.

"Where are you going?"

"I need my phone so I can show you something." She digs through her purse and sits beside me, and opens a picture."

"I don't know what that is?" I squint, trying to place to make out what's on the fuzzy black-and-white printed photo.

She takes my hand, placing it on her lower belly. "That is our baby."

I'm silent, processing her words and how I feel about them.

"Ever," she speaks my name softly.

I get on my knees between her legs and lay my ear on her belly. "Our baby." I choke back tears that are lodged in my throat, full of emotions I didn't know I was capable of having.

She runs her hands through my hair. "Yes, our baby."

"This is the most terrifying thing I've ever experienced," I whisper. "What if I'm not good enough?"

She laughs. "Are you kidding me? You've lived a horrific childhood, and you're going to let a peanut-size baby scare you. And as far as not being good enough, there's no one else in the world I'd rather raise my child with. You are going to be the most protective father alive."

"If I'll be around to raise…him or her?" He lifts a quizzical brow.

"That answer is in an envelope I've been carrying around with me. I wanted us to learn the sex of our baby together."

"Is it in your purse?"

She nods and smiles.

I bounce to my feet and pick up her bag, handing it to her, then sit next to her with my arm around her shoulders. She presses her lips together and opens the sealed envelope, taking out a tri-folded piece of paper. Holding it between us, she unfolds it.

I stare at it for a long moment before I can speak. "A daughter." I inhale my hushed words.

"We're having a little girl," she squeals, then settles in my lap. "I know I've had a lot more time to think about this than you, but if it was going to be a girl, I wanted to know what you thought about naming her Ella?"

"After my mother," I whisper.

"She deserves her name to be handed down for

raising a man like you." Her fingertips brush against my forehead.

"I'd like that. Very much."

"Me too." She kisses me sweetly.

I get her to her feet. "Before you turn that kiss into something more heated, you and our daughter need to eat. And, I have to admit, I'm starving." I pick up the bag of food.

"There weren't a lot of choices at the small store. I thought I'd make breakfast for dinner." She digs into the bag and takes out a carton of six eggs, bacon, and bread.

"Right now, I'll eat anything."

She opens the fridge and snorts. "You call this food?" She pulls out a six-pack of beer and a fresh log of pepperoni.

"The store didn't have anything stronger, and the pepperoni reminded me of you and your pizza joint."

"Fair enough." She laughs. "You find a pan, and I'll crack open the eggs."

"God, I'd love for our lives to feel this normal."

"It will soon enough, and then you'll complain about how boring our lives will be."

"My life with you will never be labeled boring." I

use finger quotes. "Besides, I could use a much calmer life."

"We're having a baby. It will be full of chaos," she beams.

As she cooks, I touch her as often as I can. I don't want her out of my reach. I take down plates, and she piles the food on them. I'm not sure if we're both so hungry we are at a loss for words or if we're both so hungry for each other we inhale our food.

When she takes the last bite of her eggs and drops her fork, I stand, offering her my hand. Her cheeks turn a pretty shade of blush, and her eyes darken. "Where are you taking me?"

"Outside on the deck where we made love before. I had my staff drop off blankets and towels after we left here. Condoms too." I grin.

"Well, you won't be needing those any longer."

I spin to look at her. "Is this okay? Am I going to hurt our daughter?"

She roars. "You're well endowed, but you're not going to hurt her."

"Good, because this is going to be rough." I lean down and toss her over my shoulder, and she laughs harder, swatting me in the ass. I stomp to the back deck and set her on her feet and drag a blanket from an outdoor cabinet, and spread it on the ground.

"How fast can you get naked?"

We start stripping out of our clothes at the same time, and I get hung up, whipping off my belt. "Is that fast enough for you?" She bites my bottom lip and unbuttons my pants.

"You're beautiful." I nip at her chin, and she yanks off my pants and boxers.

"Back at you, mister." She wraps her long fingers around my shaft.

"I'd be careful. You're playing with an explosive." I chuckle low in my throat.

She kneels down, sucking me into her mouth all the way to the root. I hiss for control. She repeats the process with her sexy, darkened gaze on my emerald greens until I can take no more. Pushing her down to the ground with my body, I hover over her, resting my weight on my elbows. "My turn," I hum and kiss my way downward until I'm settled between her thighs. "You're so ready for me." I swipe a finger between her folds.

"I was rip-roaring and ready the moment you walked from behind that fridge." She shudders when I insert two fingers, crisscrossing them deep inside her, then replace my fingers with my tongue. She bucks her hips and clings to my hair, pushing me deeper, climaxing within seconds, spilling into my mouth. I lap her up and push her to the brink again, and she pulses around me, riding out another orgasm.

I sit back with my feet under me and dig my fingers into her hips, drawing her into a sitting position above me, and I slowly sink her onto my steel-hard cock. "You feel so good." I clench my teeth.

She places her hands on my shoulders and arches her back, rocking her hips. I concentrate on ravaging her nipple to stave off the sensation of my dick buried in her warmth.

"Yes," she cries when I tweak her peaked nipple between my teeth.

Trailing my fingers down her spine to her ass, I lift her all the way off my cock and then bolt my hips upward while slamming her hips downward.

She moans loudly, and I do it again, fighting for my own control. She shifts her hips seating me deeper, and I lose the battle, growling her name. "Noa!" My orgasm seems to be unending, and as soon as I'm done, I'm ready again. I don't pull out of her. We move together as one, and I ease her onto the blanket and take my time making love to her as if it will be the last time. I pray it's not, but I don't ever want to forget this moment in time between us. She came looking for me, risking her own life. The love I have for this woman is overwhelming, and now… there's our baby. I will protect both of them at all costs.

"I don't ever want to leave this place." She kisses the center of my chest.

"You'd leave Essex to live here with me?"

She giggles. "Why do you sound surprised?"

"No one has sacrificed the things they love for me." I run my hand the length of her hair.

"You are more important to me than where I live."

I roll her onto her back, and I rest on my elbows. "You did that already with Drake. You hated New York, yet that's where the two of you settled."

"I've had many nights contemplating my life. You've made my heart full in a way Drake never did. He made choices based on his needs, and I let him because I thought it would make him happy. I've learned I wasn't enough for him and vice versa. You, Ever Christianson, and this baby growing inside of me are all I need. Where you go, I go."

"In the future, that might be true. You can't stay here as long as Victor is out there somewhere hunting for you."

"He doesn't know about this place, and I can't go home."

"He's resourceful. Eventually, he'll find out about this property, and I can't have you here when he does."

"What are you going to do?"

"I can't sit back and let him find you. I'm going to go after him."

"Why don't you let Ricco help you? I promise he's on your side."

"I'll consider it." I stand, extending my hand toward her. "Let's go for a swim."

"I don't have a suit or any change of clothes."

"We don't need any."

"It's broad daylight. People will see us." She sits, covering her breasts with her hand.

"Let them." I wiggle my fingers, and she smiles.

"Alright." She takes my hand, getting up. "Race you," she says, dashing off, and I gladly chase her

21 EVER

The day sinks into night, and I order from Uber Eats to deliver a steak dinner, complete with sweet potatoes and a salad, along with a bottle of sparkling cider.

"Since you can't have wine, I thought we'd celebrate with this." I hold up the bottle.

"Which thing are we celebrating?" She wraps her arms around my waist with her chin between my shoulder blades.

"Us and our daughter."

"I'll drink to both." She releases me, and I pour the liquid into paper cups.

"To Ella." She raises her cup.

"Ella Ines Christianson." I tip mine to hers.

"My mother's name?"

"For the same reason you wanted to use my mother's. She raised a remarkable woman that I'm madly in love with."

"One day soon, I hope you'll get to meet my parents."

"I've never been the type of guy that women bring home to the family," I grunt.

"That's because they never made it past your bed," she snorts.

"Yet"—I snatch her hand—"somehow you did."

"It was those emerald-colored eyes that drew me in," she hums.

"Was that all?" I smirk.

"It couldn't have been the charm," she teases, then snaps her fingers. "It was the bad boy appeal."

"Then you won the prize." I laugh hard.

"I've always been a bit of an overachiever." She winks, scrunching her adorable nose.

She takes a sip of her drink, and a yawn slips onto her face.

"You're tired. What do you say to a hot shower, and we turn in early?"

"It has been a rather long day."

"You go get the shower warm, and I'll take care of this mess."

Her chair scrapes the floor, and she sways her hips over to me and sits in my lap. "I love you."

"I love you too. Both of you." I lean my head down and kiss her stomach.

"I'll see you upstairs."

I clean up the kitchen and grab towels from outside, wishing now I'd had my staff fully stock this house. Climbing the stairs, I enter the bathroom with Noa already in the shower.

"Don't you dare scrub one part without me," I deepen my voice to sound commanding.

"That's a little hard to do with no soap."

"I'll have all the supplies we need as soon as this ordeal is over."

She changes positions with me, and the water rains down on my body. "Do you think you should contact Chief Bentley and let him know that Victor has the journal?"

"All I know is that right now, I want to forget about the rest of the world for one night. I'll deal with what comes next tomorrow."

MORNING COMES WAY TOO SOON. I roll over to find my bed empty. Fear surges like a tsunami in my veins. "Noa!" I scramble to my feet, jump into my jeans and run barefoot down the stairs. "Noa!" I search the bottom floor. The sliders are open, so I run outside. She's plodding the length of the deck with her phone to her ear.

"Papa, slow down. I can't understand you when you're talking so fast." She listens for a moment. "Sofia's been working long days. Perhaps she overslept." She's quiet again. "Use the key under the flowerpot to get in and call me back." She hangs up.

"What's going on? And you seriously keep a key under a flowerpot?" I narrow my eyes.

"Sofia was supposed to meet our father for breakfast this morning. She never showed up."

"He should be worried," I growl, clenching my teeth.

"Why do you say that?"

"If Victor went looking for you and only found Sofia, he'd use her to get to you."

"I'm calling Ricco."

"Don't alarm him until your father calls you back."

"But if he…"

I fold her in my arms. "I know, but he won't kill her. It's me he truly wants. She's just the tool to get to me. He knows if he harms her, his game is over."

"Will any of us ever be safe?" She peers into my eyes.

"Not until Victor is no longer an issue. I could leave the country, but he'd still come after you to draw me out."

"What if we let him find me?"

"You mean set him up?"

She nods.

"No way in hell am I letting him anywhere near you." I drop my arms to my sides.

"You're willing to risk your life for me, but I'm not allowed to do the same?"

"We're not talking just your life anymore." My gaze dips to her belly. "Besides, this is my mess, and I'll die cleaning it up. If I can't be a free man, you, me, and this baby will never have a life together. You'll be the one that has to disappear so he can't find you. So, my choices are limited. I find him and kill him, or he kills me."

"I don't like the sound of any of that." Her phone rings. "Papa," she answers and listens, then all the color drains from her face.

"What did he find?"

She covers the receiver. "The front door was open when he arrived, and it looked like there was a struggle. Sofia's car is there, but she's not."

"Tell him I'm going to find her." My hands clench at my sides.

She tells him, trying to calm him down before she hangs up.

"Call Ricco. Give him the address and tell him to come here alone."

Her hand shakes as she calls him.

I connect with Luca and get an earful of his anger laced with worry that I haven't contacted him. Updating him on my whereabouts, I ask that he arrives with Ricco at this location but make a pit stop first, gathering items Noa will need to stay in this house. "Make sure to get her plenty of fresh fruit and vegetables and a couple of cartons of orange juice." I recall seeing a few bottles in the bag she purchased yesterday. When Noa is preoccupied discussing the situation with Ricco, I step off the deck and walk to the shoreline, calling Victor.

"I was wondering how long it would take for you to reach out to me." He laughs. "Word travels fast when someone you love is missing."

"Let her go! It's me you want."

"What would be the fun in that? You've ruined your family's life and mine. There has to be some sort of payback. I tell you what, though, I will make an exchange."

"What is it you want?"

"Noa for this hot little feisty number in my car. The bitch clawed my face."

"You won't get your hands on Noa, and if you hurt her sister, you'll know what pain really is," I growl.

"That should terrify me coming from someone who learned the art of torture firsthand from his own monstrous father, but it doesn't. I've got the upper hand with Sofia and the journal, which would make for good kindling."

"Tell me where you are. I'll come unarmed, and you can do with me what you will, but you'll free her."

"I'll be in touch," he snarks, disconnecting our call.

"Damn it!" I clench my jaw.

"Was that Victor?" I didn't hear Noa walk up behind me.

"Yes." I swallow hard.

"Does he have Sofia?"

I nod, rocking my jaw back and forth.

"You agreed to exchange yourself for her." Tears pool in her eyes.

"It's the only way."

"He'll kill you."

"I know."

She runs into my arms, sobbing. "There has to be another way."

"Not if you want your sister back."

"I want both! Her back and you alive!" Her cries turn to screams of agony.

"Listen to me. I want you and Sofia to go back to Essex and forget about me. Love our child enough for the two of us, but when you tell our daughter about me, could you leave out all the bad parts. Tell her how much I loved her mother."

She slaps me repeatedly in the chest. "No! No! No!"

I hold her tight, kissing the top of her head. "You're going to be alright, and so is your sister. I'll meet Victor alone, and he's going to let her go."

"You can't go alone. Take Ricco with you." She pulls back, wiping her tears.

"I can't. He'll kill him too. Victor is ruthless and will show no mercy."

She covers her ears with her hands. "Stop! I can't listen anymore to you being resolved to die. None of this can be real. It's all just a bad dream that I'm going to wake up from at any moment. First, I lose my husband, only to find out it was at the hands of your family. Now I'm supposed to lose you too! You have to find a way to fight him." She sticks her chin in the air. "If not for my sake, then for your daughter."

"Don't you get it!" I run my hand through my hair. "I am doing this for the two of you. I'm sorry you ever got involved with me. It was something beyond both of our control, and I wish like hell I didn't love you, but I do! If my family or Victor gets wind of the fact that you are carrying my baby, they'll never leave you alone. They'll hunt you down, take your life, and then our baby will grow up with those monsters."

"Your family is behind bars. There's nothing more they can do to us."

"If I can't retrieve the journal to prove all the things my father has done and all the people he's paid off to steer clear of his organization, I'll be the one behind bars."

"Then we'll take it from Victor."

"It's not that simple."

"I'm not giving up and losing you. I'll find a way." She trots through the white sand back to the house.

22 NOA

Silence sprinkled the room between us until Ricco pulled into the driveway, followed by Luca. I run out of the house and into Luca's arms, knowing he'll feel the same pain I do.

"I brought you some things you'll need," he says next to my ear.

"He's going to sacrifice himself for me," I cry quietly.

"I know, and as much as I dislike it, I wouldn't expect anything else from him."

"We can't let him," I protest. "The four of us can come up with a plan."

"You'll be part of no such plan," Ricco speaks loudly. "I already could lose my job by being here without backup. I'm not involving you any more beyond what you previously have been."

Ever slowly moves toward us and stares at Ricco.

Ricco steps up to him and extends his hand. "It's nice to finally meet you."

Ever blinks a few times. "I'm at a bit of a disadvantage here. You know about me, and I knew nothing of you until a few days ago."

"Yes, I've known who you are for several years."

"Were you one of the agents that turned your head to the things that were done to me by my father?" He tilts his head to the side.

"No. I'm appalled at the way your case has been handled, and I want nothing more than to rectify it. I know you're not an innocent man, but the man we know as our father is a monster, and I want to help you get rid of him once and for all. You deserve a chance at the life your mother was trying to give you. My mother was lucky enough to get away from him without him knowing her secret. Otherwise, my life could easily be yours."

Ever finally reaches out, taking Ricco's hand that had remained in place. "Then let's put a plan in motion to make that happen."

A tiny bit of relief washes over me, thinking he's

not just giving up. Ever helps Luca carry bags into the house after they've greeted one another with a manly hug and whispered a few words between them.

I take Ricco by the arm and walk him into the house. "Ever is planning on meeting Victor alone. You can't let that happen."

"He's spoken with Victor?" He raises a concerned brow.

"Yes. Victor said he'd be in contact. He only agreed to let Sofia go in exchange for Ever. I want my sister back unharmed, but he can't just walk into Victor's arms without backup."

"Let me talk to him."

After the bags are carried inside, the men gather around the oversized breakfast bar. The three of them stare at one another, and then Ever turns to me. "Why don't you go put away some of the things that Luca brought you?"

I narrow my eyes, angry that he doesn't want me to be part of the conversation, but I relent so the three of them can work together. "Fine," I snap, picking up a few of the bags, then hurry up the stairs. I quickly change out of the clothes I've been wearing from the bag Luca brought, into a simple blouse and skirt. Then tiptoe halfway down so I can eavesdrop on their conversation.

"I spoke with Victor. He confirmed that he, in fact, has Sofia. I don't believe he'll harm her because he wants me. He has the journal too." Ever is trying to keep his voice low, but I can still clearly hear him.

"Did he tell you where he was?" Ricco asks.

"No. He said he'd be in touch, but from the background noises I was hearing, he was driving. He'll call when he gets to wherever he plans on taking Sofia. I have to go alone, or this won't play out like we need it to."

"Going alone is not an option," Luca pipes up.

"He's right. Once you know his location, I can go in unseen," Ricco states.

"I can't risk it. There is too much at stake. I'll text you where the location is once I'm there. I'll make the exchange with Sofia and send her in your direction. After it's a done deal and she's clear, you can come in and either save me or retrieve my body. Either way, don't let Victor leave with the journal, or it's all for not. Even if I'm dead, my father will seek revenge on anyone connected to me. He'll find out Noa is carrying my child, and he'll kill her to take my daughter away from her just like he did my mother."

My heart aches for him. By doing no more than loving this man, I've led him down a path with very few choices.

"I suspected as much about your mother from your file. I'm so sorry for your loss." Ricco's tone is filled with sympathy.

I hear a sniff but no words.

"What can I do to help?" Luca's voice is heavy.

"Stay here, and don't let Noa out of your sight. When this is all over, if I don't make it back, I've left you enough money to work for her the rest of your days."

"I don't want your money. I'll take care of her because I love you like a son, and she's your family. Our family."

I hear footsteps on the tile and then what sounds like them clapping each other on the back in a hug.

"He's the father Ever deserved," I whisper.

"I can still have a few men on standby to get Sofia, and I can be close by to get Victor."

"It's my way or no way," Ever says stubbornly.

"I'll respect your decision but know that I'm coming in with guns blazing as soon as Sofia is a safe distance away," Ricco tells him.

"I'm counting on it," Ever chuckles.

A phone rings, and Ever answers it, placing it on speakerphone. "Victor."

"I've decided to take you up on your offer. I want nothing to do with this hellcat. I'll text you the address of where to meet me. Be there at seven p.m. sharp, or I'll take the liberty of putting her down. Don't forget, come alone. If I see anyone other than your face, I'll torch the place with her and the journal locked inside."

"I understand the terms. I'll be there." Ever's tone is firm.

"Was that him?" I ask as if I don't already know.

"Yes. We've set up a time and meeting place," he scrolls through his phone and shows the address to Ricco.

"I'll pull it up." He unzips the bag he brought in, takes out his laptop, and puts it on the breakfast bar. Within a few minutes, his screen is lit up with a map. "According to this, it's an abandoned apartment complex in a seedy part of town."

"I know this place. My father purchased it and ran off all the tenants. He wanted the property for a future development plan. It fell through when the city officials condemned it and decided not to renovate the area."

"I bet that pissed him off." Luca grins.

"It's been sitting empty ever since. He couldn't unload it on anyone."

"So, Victor knows there will be no one around," Ricco says.

"Other than a few homeless people," Luca adds.

"We've got approximately three hours, including drive time." Ricco peers at his watch. "I need to check in with my superiors. Don't worry, I won't tell them anything."

"You'll lose your job," I chime into the conversation.

He braces his hand on my shoulder. "Once this is over, I will have completed my goal of working for the FBI. Besides, I have a job at a busy pizza joint outside of Boston. I have a thing for one of the owners." He winks, and I hug him.

"Thank you."

"I'll gather some weapons. What do you need?" he asks Ever.

"Nothing. I'm going in empty-handed. Victor will search me, and if I have a weapon, the exchange won't happen."

"I'll hole up here." He points to the screen. "It's far enough away he won't have eyes on me, and Sofia can make it to this spot on foot."

"Alright." Ever blows out a puff of air.

"I'm going to head out. Noa can give you my number. If anything changes, call me."

"I will." Ever walks him to the door.

"How are you holding up?" Luca's eyes are filled with empathy.

"The best I can, considering the awful circumstances."

Ever returns to the kitchen and gives Luca a look.

Luca clears his throat. "I'm going to go check out the view on the deck and perhaps put my feet in the sand."

Once he's through the glass doors, Ever takes my hand. "Promise me you won't leave this house. I need to know that you're safe here with Luca."

"I don't want to let you go."

"That's not a promise, Noa." He tips my chin up to look him in the eyes.

"I promise."

"Thank you." He kisses me. "If there is any way possible, I'm coming back to my girls."

"You better." I wrap my hands around his neck and draw his lips back to mine. "She needs to know how much I love her father."

He presses his forehead to mine. "I love you so much it hurts. I wish I had time to make love to you one more time, but I don't."

"I'm not opposed to a quickie." I nip his bottom lip, and he snakes his hand under my blouse, cupping my breast. "It would only show you how much I want you, not how much I love you."

"I'll take what I can get." I unzip his jeans and stroke his already-hardening cock.

He lifts me up, sets me on the bar, and hikes my skirt up my thighs. "I like it when you wear no panties," he hisses when he touches my bare skin. "You're so damn wet already."

"That's the effect you have on me whenever we are in the same room," I run my tongue along the rim of his ear.

Grabbing my hips, he pulls me to the edge of the bar and then eases inside me inch by glorious inch. "I love the feel of you," I rasp and thrust him deeper into me.

He locks his hands on either side of my face and steels his eyes with mine while he thrusts in and out. "I love you, Noa Sutton, and don't ever forget it."

His words bring me to an instant climax, and I bite my bottom lip so that I don't scream. He grunts and spills inside me as our breaths mingle together, and then his tongue dances with mine.

"I want you to know that in the short time I've loved you, you are my world. You saved me from a life I wanted no part of. I don't regret loving you, and I never will."

"You have to come back to me because as much as I tried when I left New York, I can't imagine a life after you."

23 EVER

I turn into the deserted edge of town smattered with rundown, vacant buildings. Tents housing homeless people are gathered in one spot around a building that housed a motel at one point in time. The apartment complex is fenced off with a keep-out sign hanging on with one screw from the metal fencing that surrounds it. As I park, I see Victor's car. He gave me the location but not where in the five-story building I should meet him.

"I'm here," I call him. "Where exactly would you like me to meet you?"

"Let's play a little game of cat and mouse, shall we," he cackles.

"I'm not in to playing games Victor. Just tell me where the hell you are!" I growl.

"What's the matter, Ever? Didn't you ever get to enjoy the game of hide-and-go-seek? Oh, that's right, it was hard to hide when you were living in a cage like an animal. As far as I see it, that cage was much too large for a rat," he spits out the T.

He's baiting me. "I won't have a problem finding you. Your stench will give you away," I bite back.

"I failed to share with you earlier that you're on a time limit. Sofia has twenty minutes left before you hear a kaboom." He laughs, hanging up.

Bolting out of my car, I assess the colorful graffitied exterior for the quickest way inside. The door falls off its hinges when I jar it open, and I'm greeted by a rat skittering through debris left by squatters. I step over broken glass from blown-out windows to move through the entryway leading to a hallway. Crusty paint and rippled wallpaper hang loosely with its remnants on the old stained green-bean-colored carpet. Flies buzz around me as I open a creaking door. I cover my nose to avoid the smell of urine and feces. Ragged holes are in various places in the walls bleeding mouse-chewed insulation. With each door I open, I stop and listen, praying to hear a noise from Sofia instead of the sounds of the building shifting from the draft of broken windows.

Closing my eyes for a moment, I try to recall the

things I've heard my father say in his hostage situations about where to hide the victim.

"NEVER ON THE FIRST FLOOR. *You don't want to make it too easy. They'll waste their time on the middle floors while the clock ticks. Always have them on the roof."*

IT SICKENS me to know these are the things I've learned from my father. I don't bother with the elevator, knowing that it's broken. Hauling ass up the stairs two at a time, I don't stop until I'm on the top floor and find the roof access. Slowly, I open the door. The thick gray clouds have made it darker than normal at this time of evening. I hear a whimper as soon as I hit the flat rooftop.

"Sofia!" I yell, running toward her.

She's gagged and tied to a flagpole mounted near the edge of the building. There's a box at her feet. "I've got you," I tell her, releasing the gag from her mouth.

"It's a bomb," she cries.

I stoop, opening the lid of the box. "It's alright. I know how to disarm it." Another tidbit I learned from my old man. I disconnect it, and the timer stops counting down. "I'm going to get you out of here." I work on freeing the knots from around her wrist.

"Listen to me very carefully," I whisper next to her ear, not knowing where Victor is hiding. "Ricco is waiting for you a half mile east of this building. You're going to use the fire escape to get out of here. It's old and rusted, so be careful. When your feet hit the pavement, run as fast as you can to the back of the property, staying out of the field. Go around it, and once you've cleared the area, I want you to move as fast as you can, don't stop until you're in Ricco's arms."

"What about you?" She rubs her rope-burnt wrists.

"Don't worry about me. Just focus on getting out of here."

"I see you found her," Victor says, wielding a gun and coming out of his hiding place from a standup air conditioning vent that has a full-size opening. "And, from the looks of it, your father taught you well." He glances at the box.

"I'm here now. She's leaving." I stand in front of her protectively.

"Why should I keep my word to a lying piece of shit like you? I don't know why your father didn't see right through your bullshit! Trusting you was his downfall, and I'm not going down with them." He yanks the journal free from the back of his pants. "I'd bet you'd kill for this."

I speak low and firmly. "Sofia, I'm going to shield you with my body as you walk over to the fire escape. Remember what I told you." She inches a few feet, and he squeezes the trigger, drilling the pole with the bullet. Sofia goes to her knees, covering her ears.

"You don't want to do this. We had a deal. Let her go. I'm unarmed and alone." I put my arms straight out to my side and slowly turn in a circle. "She's got nothing to do with this." I help her to her feet and stay in front of her until she reaches the stairs. "Go, and don't look back," I tell her.

The fire escape shifts and sways under the weight of her feet, and she hangs on tight to the railing. "Take your time." I prompt her to keep moving.

"You're such the hero," Victor taunts me.

I scan the area for anything I can use for a weapon. "If you're going to kill me, go ahead and do it."

"You're not getting off that easily," he tisks, sneering his nose. "In turning in your family, you've put the nail in your own coffin. This book holds all your misdeeds too."

"I never claimed I was an innocent man." I glance over my shoulder to see that Sofia is halfway down the ladder.

"You know you were correct about your mother. Your father ordered her death. It's all in this book, not just timeframes that would link him to the crime. I'm assuming you didn't read the entire thing. Not only did he kill her, he killed her sister too."

My mother had a sister?

"It assured him you'd have no other place to go once your mother was out of the picture. He even had a written plan to kill that woman of yours if you didn't come to see the error of your ways. If you hadn't convinced him, she'd be dead by now."

"What's your point in telling me any of this if you plan on killing me anyway?"

He strides toward the edge of the roof, keeping his aim on me. "Did you really think I was going to let her flee?" He moves the gun to aim downward at Sofia, and I tackle him to the ground. The journal flies to the ledge of the roof, and his gun remains in his hand. I punch him in the face repeatedly, then feel a burning sensation drill through my thigh after the sound of his gun going off. I falter to the ground with blood bubbling through my jeans. Whipping off my belt, I tighten it around my leg. When I look up, Victor is wobbling to the fire escape with blood gushing from his nose, and he leans his elbow on the edge for support taking his shot.

Relief fills me when he yells, "Shit!" I know she got away. "Run, Sofia, run," I whisper to myself and feel light-headed.

Victor's nose is bloody, and he's snarling as he stalks to me, gripping me by my shirt and dragging me over the concrete roof, slamming me against a wall.

My leg feels like it's on fire, but I refuse to scream in pain.

"It doesn't really matter. She's not the one I was after, anyway. My men will take care of the other one for me."

"You're lying. You have no men." Luca will defend her. I told him where he could find a gun hidden in the house.

"You're seriously calling me a liar?" He laughs.

"If you did, you wouldn't have left New York to kidnap her sister. You would have sat back and waited for your men to bring her to you," I spit.

"I guess you'll never really know, will you? Unless

you survive the torture I have planned for you, which I highly doubt you will."

I use the wall to help me get to my feet.

"Where the hell do you think you're going?"

"I want to see for myself that Sofia got away before I kill you."

His head falls back, clearly amused. "You and what army? You seem to forget I'm the only one holding the gun." With his free hand, he picks up the rope that he had Sofia bound with and walks toward me.

"Turn around and put your hands behind your back." When I don't comply, he lifts his foot and jabs it into my thigh.

I bite down, holding back any sound.

"Tough guy, huh? We'll see how tough you are when I cut off your fingers one by one." He swiftly raises his knee, connecting with my jaw.

I fall back, and the brick grinds into my back. Noa's face flashes before my eyes. She's holding a baby, rocking her, but the baby is blurred out. It gives me the strength I need to lunge at him again; this time, the gun flies from his hand, skidding over the concrete. The pain in my leg gives him the advantage to scramble to his feet. I limp, making it to him as a gun fires in the distance.

Victor stills, facing me, and red smears his gray shirt. He falters, and I snag him by the belt before he tumbles over the edge. "You didn't come alone," he gurgles.

"You said it was a game. I thought I'd bring my own player."

"You lied." His eyes start to bulge.

"You did say I was a liar."

The door crashes open, and Ricco is in black attire, wearing a vest and a holster with his arms outstretched, gripping his weapon. "Don't let go of him," he barks. "I'm taking him in."

"He deserves to die. If he goes to prison, he'll only get out, and next time we won't see him coming."

Victor coughs. "He's right. I'll kill all of you."

"Ever," Ricco says my name as a warning. "Let the justice system handle this."

"Like they did for me? They watched my father torment me as a child to use me as a pawn," I seethe.

"That doesn't make this right. Let me take him in."

I gnaw his words to death and think of Noa. "He said he has men going after Noa as we speak."

He gets on his radio and requests a team be deployed to the West Hampton Dunes house immediately. "Luca will not let anything happen to her."

I steady him on his feet and let go, taking a couple of steps back and lifting my hands in the air. "Take him," I state, staring Victor straight in the face.

"I'm not going to prison!" he yells and launches himself at me. A round of gunfire has his body convulsing, flailing him backward. He teeters on the edge and then falls like a mannequin five stories to the ground.

"I have Sofia loaded in a chopper over the hill. I'll have them fly you to the Dunes." He picks up the journal. "I'll see to it that this gets into the proper hands. You need to go to the hospital and have that bullet removed."

I peer over the edge making sure Victor is dead. "It will have to wait until I know Noa is safe."

"Go." He waves me off. "I'll take care of things here, and I'll have one of my associates meet you on the ground to tend to your leg."

"Thank you for saving my life." I press my lips together firmly, then hit the stairs ignoring the shooting pain, not stopping until I hop on the chopper. Ricco already informed them via his radio where to take me.

Sofia clings to my neck. "I was so scared."

"Victor said you gave him a hard time. I saw the scratches on his face."

"I wasn't going to let him take me without a fight."

"You did good."

"Noa! Where is she?" She's suddenly frantic.

"She's with Luca. We're headed there now."

"Ricco? Why isn't he on board?"

"Victor is dead. He's staying behind to deal with the fallout."

"Did…" she stammers, "you kill him?"

"No. Ricco shot him, defending me."

She clings to me again. "Thank God you're okay." Then she gets a good look at me. "Your leg."

I fasten her into her seat, and we take off. I don't tell her about the possible danger Noa is in because it still could be a lie from Victor. I slowly ease off the pressure of the belt. "It stopped bleeding. That's a good sign."

24 NOA

"The waiting is killing me," I whine, sitting next to Luca on a makeshift couch built from pillows he purchased.

"It's the worst part. When Ever was a teenage boy, I used to sit and wait for him all the time, worried when he was late that something happened to him."

"Was he a handful? I bet he had girls lined up at his door."

"Neither. I think he was afraid to get out of line because of his father. I recall the first task his father gave him was to evict a single mom and her infant son from their home. His father wanted her land to build a casino. Ever was sick for days afterward. He crawled in the back seat of my car and asked if I'd loan him some money. I didn't bother asking what he needed it for because he never asked anything of me, so I figured whatever it was, he needed it."

"Did you find out what it was for?"

"He took the money and opened a bank account for the woman, paid her lease on a new apartment for three months, and stocked her fridge. That's when I knew all the beatings he had received didn't truly change him. He was good, caught in a bad world. He paid me back every cent."

"I'm surprised you let him."

"I wasn't going to take away the pride he felt for doing something good for another human being. As far as women being lined up at his doorstep, you're right, but he never connected with any of them."

"I bet you've been his saving grace." I nudge him with my shoulder. "Why haven't you ever married and had a family of your own?"

"I almost married once, but she wanted me to move to her hometown in Connecticut."

"Why didn't you?"

"Because it would have left Ever with no one on his side."

"You gave up your life for him."

"Quite the contrary. He gave me purpose in life."

"Do you ever regret your decision?"

"The only thing I regret is not being able to help Ever escape his family. I thought about taking him and disappearing with him several times, but the consequences he would have faced once he was found was too great of a risk."

"I don't know if he's told you or not, but he loves you very much."

"And I him."

The crunching of gravel has Luca on his feet, tiptoeing to the window. "Go upstairs and hide," he whispers.

I run to the top of the stairs and see him open the door underneath the stairwell, pulling out a rifle. I move to the master bedroom, looking for somewhere to hide. Shutting the door, I lock it and shuffle to the closet. I look up seeing the access door to the attic. I jump when I hear a gunshot and grab the rope to the door, pulling it down. Climbing up, I tug the door closed behind me and crawl through the narrow space. What's left of the day is dimly lighting the space through a round window. I make my way to it so I can look outside. Keeping low, I peek out. I see two men dressed in dark clothing wearing ski masks hunched down in a row of bushes lined along the driveway. One man moves, and the rifle goes off again, hitting him in the shoulder. He falls to the ground, then rolls over, shooting his weapon.

"Luca," I cry.

While he's shooting, the other man moves closer, hiding behind Luca's car. He fires his gun, and the other man gets to his feet and runs toward the house.

"I have to help him." I scamper back to the attic opening, and as I push it open, I gasp. Luca startles me. "Come on." I extend my hand.

He climbs the steps and quietly shuts the door.

"How did you know I was in here?"

"The bedroom door was locked, so I could only assume you'd be in here somewhere."

"Who are they?"

"They must be Victor's associates."

"Do you have your phone on you?"

He pats his pockets. "Yes." He immediately dials Ever's number. "It goes directly to voicemail."

"Hang up and call Ricco."

"I don't have his number."

"Give it to me." I squeeze my eyes shut, trying to recall his phone number. I tap it in, hoping it's right.

"Hello," he answers.

"Ricco, it's Noa. There are two men with guns outside. They may be inside by now."

"I have men headed in your direction, and Ever is in a chopper. They should be landing shortly."

"Ever is alive." I breathe.

"Yes, and Victor is dead. I have the journal, so Ever will be a free man. Stay hidden until he gets there."

"We'll try and hold them off."

The crashing of a door being broken has me hanging up and holding my breath.

"We know you're in here somewhere!" a man's deep voice echoes through the walls.

Luca readies the rifle toward the attic opening, sitting in front of me.

Light floods the attic when the door opens. Footsteps pound the small wooden stairs, and a headlight blinds us. Luca fires, barely missing whoever it is. Before he can get another shot off, the guy pulls the trigger, and Luca falls back into my arms.

"No!" I scream. Wrapping my arms around him, I hold pressure to his chest.

The man marches toward me and grabs me by the hair, and I have no choice but to let go of Luca. "Please don't do this. He's going to die!" I wail.

He drags me down the stairs, and then his body springs backward, falling to the ground. I look up to see an FBI agent holding his gun.

"Are you okay?" he asks, looking me squarely in the face.

"Yes, but Luca isn't." I scramble up the stairs.

His eyes are half hooded, and he moans when I place both my hands on his chest to stop the bleeding. "Don't you dare die on me," I cry, reminiscent of the night Drake was murdered. "I'm not going to let you. I need you, and so does Ever." My tears spill on his cheek.

I hear the agent calling for a life flight, and a few seconds later, Ever is at my side. "He goes in the chopper," he barks to the agent. He cradles Luca in his arms and limps, carrying him down the stairs out the front of the house.

Sofia bolts through the door and into my arms. "Thank God you're alright." She looks battered, and mascara has dried to her cheeks.

"I'm so sorry," I weep on her shoulder. "I thought I'd never see you again."

"I'm here, and I'm okay. Did they hurt you?"

"No, but Luca…" I gulp. "He was shot in the chest saving me."

We step out on the porch to see the helicopter take flight. "I don't see Ever."

"He went with him, ma'am," an agent tells me.

"Do you know where they are taking him?"

"If they can stabilize him, he'll go into the Boston trauma center. If not, they'll take him to the nearest hospital."

I run back inside and grab Luca's keys he set on the bar. "We have to go."

Sofia is on my heels. "We don't even know where."

"We'll find out on the way. Call Ricco." I toss her Luca's phone. "He'll be able to find out."

I speed down the narrow road of the island to the mainland as Sofia talks to Ricco. "He'll call me as soon as he locates them." She reaches out, touching my hand on the steering wheel.

"I'm so scared," I admit, my lip trembling. "If Luca dies…"

"Ever is going to do everything he can to not let that happen. You should have seen him in action. He disarmed the bomb and—"

"There was a bomb?" My voice rises, and I take my eyes off the road.

"Victor was playing a wicked game. He knew

Ever would be able to stop it. He told me so himself when he was setting the timer."

"It should have been me, not you."

"It shouldn't have been either one of us, but I'm glad it was me and not you. From the way he spoke, he wouldn't have let you live."

Luca's phone rings, and she snaps it up. "Ricco." She puts him on speakerphone, knowing I'd want to hear what he's about to say.

"They landed at North Shore Medical Center."

I stifle a gulp. "That means he wasn't stable enough to make the flight to Boston."

"I spoke to Ever briefly. He's in surgery as we speak."

Sofia pulls up the built-in GPS system on the dash. "We're approximately an hour out, depending on how fast Noa drives, and currently, we're going ninety miles an hour."

WE ARRIVE at the hospital emergency room parking lot, and we rush through the doors, stopping at the desk to ask where the surgical waiting room is located.

We anxiously ride the elevator to the third-floor

waiting room and check in with the lady manning the desk. "We're looking for Ever Christianson," Sofia tells her.

The lady pushes her glasses closer to her eyes and scrunches her nose. "Wait here for just a moment." She steps to the side and makes a phone call speaking in a hushed voice. "Someone will be with you in a minute." She ushers us to chairs.

"I don't understand what's going on." My heart pounds in my ears.

"I'm going to ask her about Luca." Sofia stands, and a man wearing a white jacket and surgical scrub hat walks into the waiting room.

"Are you the family of Mr. Christianson?"

"Yes," I answer without hesitation.

"He's been taken into surgery to remove the bullet in his leg. He passed out in the waiting room from the amount of blood he lost. He's lucky he was here."

"Is he going to be alright?" Sofia asks him, wrapping her arms around my shoulders.

"The bleeding has stopped, and I've ordered a couple units of blood to replace what he lost. As soon as it's infused, I'll remove the bullet. He'll be fine."

"And Luca?" I ask.

"He was in grave condition when he arrived. We're doing everything we can to save him."

Pain seers my stomach, and I double over.

"What's wrong," Sofia gasps.

"I don't know."

"Let me help you sit," the surgeon says.

"She's three months pregnant," Sofia tells him.

"I'll page the OB on call to examine you. Why don't you take her down to the maternity floor. I'll have someone keep you updated on your family members. Get her a wheelchair," he tells the lady manning the desk.

Sofia wheels me to the second floor, and I'm greeted right away by a nurse and a midwife. "You're timing was perfect. I just finished my rounds for the day," she says sweetly, helping me onto a table. "I want to do a quick sonogram if that's okay?"

I nod.

"Have you had any bleeding?"

"No."

"That's good. The doctor gave me a heads-up on your family. In all likelihood, this is stress related, but I want to take a look to make sure."

She dabs the prop with the jelly and rolls it onto my stomach. She finds the heartbeat right away. "Everything looks good. The placenta is intact, and there's no stress on the baby. I do want you to take it easy for the next couple of days and see your OB if anything changes."

"Thank you," Sofia tells her.

I lay silently in shock.

"Hey." Sofia brushes the hair from my face. "The baby is okay, and Ever will recover."

"Luca." I exhale.

"We have to have faith that he's going to make it."

"I want to go back to the waiting room."

"How about you let me get you a glass of water first, and then I'll take you."

"Okay. My mouth is really parched."

She steps into the hallway, asking where she can get water, and returns with a Styrofoam cup. "Here."

I drink it slowly so it doesn't upset my stomach any more than it already is. When I'm done, I get back in the wheelchair, and we take the elevator back to the waiting room, where it seems like forever before the surgeon comes out to talk to us.

"Mr. Christianson did well, and he's in recovery."

"Thank God." I breathe out. "When can I see him?"

"I'll have the nurse come and get you as soon as he wakes up."

"Any word on Luca?"

"The last time I enquired, he's stable but still on the operating table."

"I heard that you and the baby are okay." He smiles.

"She's going to be much better once she sees Ever." Sofia runs her hand the length of my arm.

Within an hour, a nurse is escorting us to Ever's recovery room. His eyes pop open when I enter the room, and I rush over to him, lying beside him. "You had me so scared."

"I know. I'm so sorry about everything."

"It's all over now. You're free."

"Luca," he chokes out.

"I owe him my life." I kiss his cheek.

"I need out of this bed. I'm not staying overnight." He pushes the call button.

"You need to rest. The doctor said you lost a lot of blood," Sofia interjects.

A nurse answers the call light, and Sofia shuffles her out of the room.

"Please stay. For me. We'll be able to be here when Luca is out of surgery," I plead.

"I hate hospitals."

I curl up next to him, making sure not to touch his injured leg. "You frequented them a lot when you were a kid, didn't you?"

He nods.

"The past is behind you now. I wish I could erase all your bad memories."

"It's the new ones I'm looking forward to."

"May I come in?" Ricco stands in the doorway, and I sit on the side of the bed.

"Please," Ever says.

"I wanted to be the first to tell you that you are a free man. Your past has been taken out of our database. You have a clean slate to start over."

"Thank you." I stand, hugging him.

"What's next for you?" Ever engages with him.

"I'll be turning in my resignation first thing tomorrow morning. Looks like I'll permanently be available to assist Sofia if she'll let me."

"I don't think she's going to have an issue with it," I snort. I turn around when I hear the bed squeak. "What are you doing?" Ever is sitting on the edge of the bed with his hands braced on the mattress.

"Just give me a minute." He winces getting to his feet, then straightens his spine holding out his hand to Ricco. "Thank you…brother."

"You're welcome." Instead of shaking his hand Ricco hugs him.

"I'm sorry to interrupt, but I have an update on your friend," the surgeon says, tapping on the doorframe. We collectively hold our breath. "He's out of surgery and stable."

"Can I see him?" Ever's eyes glass over with unshed tears.

"Only for a few minutes. I'll have someone bring you a wheelchair."

"Thanks, Doc." Ever sits and waits until his transportation arrives.

"I'm going to go find Sofia," Ricco states. "We'll talk later."

Ever fights me, but I help him into the wheelchair. "Stubborn man," I snark, and he laughs.

We're buzzed into the ICU, and we can see Luca through the glass doors. There is a nurse at his bedside. "The surgeon said it would be alright to see him for a few minutes," I tell her.

"He's already showing signs of waking up." She smiles.

I wheel Ever next to him, and he reaches out, covering Luca's hand. Luca's eyes slowly open, and he mumbles something. I lean over him. "Say it again."

He weakly clears his throat several times. "Ever," he rasps.

"I'm right here." Ever squeezes his hand, and Luca rolls his head to see him. "Is it over?"

"Yes, and I owe you my life for saving Noa."

Luca chuckles and coughs.

"What's so funny?" Ever scowls.

"You owe me about nine, but who's counting."

Ever busts out laughing. "I love you, man."

"I love you too, Son."

25 EVER

Two years later…

IT'S BEEN two years since my life truly began. Reflecting, I sit on our back deck overlooking the Atlantic Ocean, thinking what a lucky man I am. Noa and Ella are building a sandcastle down by the water. Both are sun-kissed from our picnic on the beach. I couldn't think of a better place to be raising children than Essex.

Sofia and Ricco have made The Fork and Dough the most popular place on the Northeast Coast to dine. People come from all over to enjoy the authentic creations of different types of pizzas. I got a taste of what restaurant life was like when Noa and I had to cover for the two of them to go on their weeklong honeymoon. It made me appreciate being in real estate. Restaurant life is definitely not in my wheelhouse.

It took a year for the trials to end with my father and Nick. They were both sentenced to life behind bars with no chance of parole. His entire organization was taken down, and anyone that wasn't arrested fled the country. Judges, mayors, and crooked cops lost their jobs, and many of them went to jail.

Every business transaction I make is on the up-and-up, and it feels so damn good. I'm truly thankful I kept my own last name, so I'm not associated with the Leones.

Noa waves at me in the distance, and Ella blows me a kiss. They are both my heart and soul. I'm so grateful Noa chose me to be her husband. We got married three days after Ella was born. I wanted to sweep Noa away to some exotic place to say our vows, but she decided that the West Hampton Dune house was all she wanted. We got married on the deck, similar to this one. In fact, she insisted this house that we built together, not far from her sister's, resembled the Dune's house but on a much smaller scale.

The first time I met her parents, her father told me off in Italian—I believe—but when he finished his tongue lashing, he kissed both sides of my face and clearly said, "Welcome to the family." I can't even begin to explain how it made me feel to be a part of something. Her father, Ricco, Luca, and I go fishing on my boat once a week, and we've bonded. Her father tried to convince me that fishing on his johnboat was better, but I converted him to think differently after the first time we took my boat out. Since then, my in-laws were treated to a two-week stint on the yacht, that I've moved further south.

My past is truly in the past. The only thing that remains is the physical scars. I wear them proudly as a symbol of what I survived. My outlook on family is very different than how I was raised. My child knows nothing but unconditional love. I'd never lay a hand on her in anger. I appreciate the years I spent with my mother trying to teach me right from wrong. I failed her for a bit, but I'd like to think she'd be proud of the man I've become. I still, to this day, miss her and wish she was here to meet Noa and Ella. She would have adored them both. Noa is the strongest, most loving person I know, and I'm thankful for her every single moment of my life. I don't believe I'd be alive if it wasn't for her, and I'll spend the rest of my life loving her.

Noa still writes her food blog, but her personal blog has exploded with followers. Telling her stories related to so many people that reached out to her. I recall tearing up reading the completed blog that is ingrained in my brain.

*THE LAST TWO years my world has consisted of one pertinent word: **After**.*

After my husband died.

After his funeral.

After I found out the man I loved had an affair.

After I found out he had a son.

After his restaurant closed.

After the apartment we shared sold.

After I met someone else...

*Then the ultimate nail on my coffin...**After Ever**.*

WAS it really the nail in my coffin, or just the beginning of a new story? I'd like to think anything is possible, even the impossible. Why should our lives be directed by a few defining moments unless it's to make us see the things we couldn't before, like what we thought love was.

Is it distinctive with one person? Or does it vary from person to person? We really don't truly know until you find that one person who settles deep within your soul.

I found my person, and he's changed me. The depth of love I feel for him is immeasurable. I don't want to admit that I can't breathe without him, that would make me weak. I've always been the strong independent type, but when I was with him, that woman no longer existed. How could I have craved him so much when he was right next to me.

I walked away from all these feelings when I left him, and now they are bottled up inside of me locked up still wondering what comes after Ever? I've found my answer...new life.

After Ever, my life truly began. I learned hard lessons about myself and him. It's amazing when you offer unconditional love to someone how much you get in return. Neither one of us is perfect, but we accept each other's flaws along with defining pasts that you work so hard to forget.

We've done it! We've moved on and created a beautiful life together. A life of love and a special gift to one another...our daughter.

Life isn't about one moment in time, it's about all of

*them and what you take away from them that matters. A word like **after** seems so blue, but in reality, it's what you do with the **after** that matters most. I've never felt more love than what came **after** losing Ever.*

"DO you mind if I join you?" Luca comes up from behind me, touching my shoulder.

"I insist." I smile.

"It's a beautiful day."

"The best. I got to spend it with my two best girls."

"They are special, and I love that Ella calls me grandpa."

"That's who you are to her and always will be."

"Have I ever thanked you for building me a house next to yours?"

"Multiple times." I chuckle.

"It's still odd not chauffeuring you around."

"Your only job for me is playing grandpa, and you're damn good at it. You spoil Ella rotten."

"Who are you kidding? She has me wrapped around her little finger." He grins.

"Our son won't be any different," Noa says, walking onto the deck with one hand holding Ella's, the other cupped under her very pregnant belly.

"Grandpa," Ella squeals, hopping into Luca's lap.

"I'm so sorry, she's full of sand." Noa scrunches her nose.

"It's quite alright. A little dirt never hurt anyone." Luca kisses Ella's pink nose.

I take Noa's hand and pull her onto my knee, kissing her belly. "How is the little rascal doing today?"

"He kept me up all night," she snorts.

"I thought that was my job," I tease, waggling my brow.

She leans down, kissing the outer shell of my ear. "You're insatiable."

"What man wouldn't be with a sexy wife like you?" I purr.

"Oh, yeah, this watermelon sitting on my lap is super sexy," she scoffs.

Luca plugs Ella's ears. "Do you two ever stop?" He smiles from ear to ear.

We look at each other in the eyes and simultaneously say, "Never Ever."

IF YOU LOVED the story of Noa and Ever, check out my other books in the Also by section at the end of this book.

Claim your FREE book when you join Kelly's Newsletter to stay up to date on what's new!

Thank you so much for reading it and please consider leaving a review.

PLAYLIST

I Can't Text You by Kyle Hume
    Without You With Me by Matt Hansen
    Better Off Without Me by Kyle Hume
    Take This Pain by Jake Banfield
    Perfect For Me by Bradley Marshall
    Paradise City by Guns N' Roses
    Dancing Queen by ABBA
    Stand by Me by Ben E King
    My Girl by the Temptations
    Ain't No Mountain High Enough by Marvin Gaye
    Dead the Day You're Gone by Matt Hansen

ABOUT THE AUTHOR

"This author has the magical ability to take an already strong and interesting plot and add so many unexpected twists and turns that it turns her books into a complete addiction for the reader." Dandelion Inspired Blog

www.kellymooreauthor.com to join newsletter and get a free book.

Armed with books in the crook of my elbow, I can go anywhere. That's my philosophy! Better yet, I'll write the books that will take me on an adventure.

My heroes are a bit broken but will make you swoon. My heroines are their own kick-ass characters armed with humor and a plethora of sarcasm.

If I'm not tucked away in my writing den, with coffee firmly gripped in hand, you can find me with a book propped on my pillow, a pit bull lying across my legs, a Lab on the floor next to me, and two kittens running amuck.

My current adventure has me living in Idaho with my own gray-bearded hero, who's put up with my shenanigans for over thirty years, and he doesn't mind all my book boyfriends.

If you love romance, suspense, military men, lots of action and adventure infused with emotion, tear-worthy moments, and laugh-out-loud humor, dive into my books and let the world fall away at your feet.

SERIES BY KELLY MOORE

Never Ever Duet

Whiskey River West

Whiskey River Road

Elite Six Series

The Revenge You Seek

The Vigilante Hitman

August Series

Epic Love Stories

For more follow me on Amazon for a detailed list of books.

Printed in Great Britain
by Amazon